A GALWAY
EPIPHANY

Also by Ken Bruen

KEN
BRUEN

A GALWAY
EPIPHANY

A Mysterious Press book
for Head of Zeus

First published in the UK in 2021 by Head of Zeus Ltd
This paperback edition first published in 2021 by Head of Zeus Ltd

9 7 5 3 1 2 4 6 8

A catalogue record for this book is available from
the British Library.

ISBN (PB): 9781838939342
ISBN (E): 9781838939311

Printed and bound in Great Britain by
CPI Group (UK) Ltd, Croydon CR0 4YY

Head of Zeus Ltd
5–8 Hardwick Street
London EC1R 4RG

WWW.HEADOFZEUS.COM

For
Paul and Martell Kennedy
and their family
Laura, John, Amy
All very special Kennedys

According to *An Leabhar Beannacht* (*The Blessed Book*), found in an old church in the 1950s and attributed to a monk in the mid-eighteenth century, there are

Seven

Epiphanies.

The monk, supposedly one Canace (old form of Kenneth), believed these epiphanies were blends of blessed curses and cursed blessings.

Kenny, as he is irreverently known by skeptics, demonstrated he was definitely Irish; he'd have to be with the skewed logic of the above statement.

For the form presented in the new edition published in 2000 by Academic Press, the epiphanies are modernized to a certain extent, and it is claimed the original was written in Latin.

The Catholic Church has banned them as being, and I quote, "*The writings of a satanic mind posing as ecclesial.*"

This could apply to a lot of the papal bulletins of late.

Whatever the case and, indeed, whatever the truth of the affair, they can, in a certain light (drunk as a skunk), seem to be instructional if not downright fucking depressing.

* * *

The first one I ever read was thus:

> *Revenge*
> *Is*
> *the*
> *Only*
> *Justice.*

By a series of wild coincidences, an English friend, here on a rare visit, saw this on the wall of my apartment and said dryly, "Francis Bacon said almost the same thing."

Which goes to show there is precious little original under the Latin sun. Or Bacon read the *Epiphanies*.

I kind of like the notion of Bacon poring over the *Epiphanies*.

Explains a lot about his wild frenzied portrait.

What the Irish in December 2018
   Might consider miracles:

> 1. Three days without rain.
> 2. Trump to resign.
> 3. A hospital bed.

The
    eighth
        of
            December.

It was a cold bright evening.

The Irish Famine Memorial to the children who died on the famine boats stood starkly against the backdrop of the ocean.

Two young people approached, aged sixteen and nine.

They'd been living, or rather barely existing, in the refugee center hastily erected on the outskirts of the Claddagh.

They'd heard bits and scraps of the young girl Celia Griffin, who died of starvation during the Irish famine.

They could understand the hunger and had seen enough of death in their travails.

The girl, a serious child, had liberated a small candle from the center's supplies and now they knelt and lit the candle for the famine child.

She whispered to the boy,

"Here's a trick I learned in Guatemala."

She drew a small metal object from beneath her thin shirt, said,

"*El espejismo azul*" (in Guatemala it was known as the blue manifestation/illusion).

As they looked up, an intense blue light shimmered above the monument, seemed to expand with lightning white streaks interwoven.

A passing American woman in her late fifties saw the moment, gasped, grabbed her iPhone, began to film.

She clearly heard the children exclaim,

"La Madonna."

The woman, though not herself Catholic, involuntarily muttered,

"Holy Mother of God!"

The clip was posted to YouTube and within twenty-four hours had gone viral.

The eighth of December, coincidentally, is the feast day of the Immaculate Conception and is fondly referred to as "Our Lady's birthday."

An epiphany of belief
Requires only
That every other area of assistance
Has been exhausted.

The Epiphany of Fire

The security guard was old.

He'd applied for the job after he'd retired from the post office.

He never expected to actually get the job but . . . the wages! The wages were shit to shinola, so he got the job.

His job was to guard an abandoned warehouse on the Newcastle Road.

His brief?

"Keep the homeless out."

He did have a conscience, but, hey, if the government didn't give a fuck, why should he? He had a chair, a radio, and a one-bar heater, plus a walkie-talkie without batteries. He'd asked the office for them and was told,

"Who are you expecting to call?"

So, no batteries.

His shift was from eight to eight, and he found those evenings were long.

To break up the monotony he'd walk the building, all two stories of it, twice; he walked it slowly, sweeping his torch across the bare floors, humming quietly to himself.

He saw some rats but rats didn't spook him. You live as long as he had, vermin were a fact of life and simply avoided.

He got into a routine.

Tea and a sandwich at ten.

Listen to the news at twelve.

Walk the building at three and five.

Snooze freely.

He'd brought some books with him but found he couldn't concentrate.

After a week of this, he filled his flask with Jameson, told himself,

1. Keeps me warm.

2. Gives me a little lift.

The second week was a lot more fun, wandering the floors, a little pissed; he felt good.

Thursday night, he was startled to hear movement on the floor above.

Muttered,

"Mighty big rat."

(He wasn't completely wrong.)

He'd just got comfortable, the heater on, thermal blanket wrapped snugly round him, the Jameson whispering happy thoughts.

"Fuck,"

He said.

He shucked the blanket off, got his torch, headed up.

On the second floor he saw the floor was wet.

"A leak?"

Then he was shocked by a wave of cold liquid thrown over him, turned, muttering,

"What the hell?"

He was soaked, saw a man in a dark track suit holding liter water bottles.

Then the smell. He lifted his arm, smelled the liquid, his heart pounding, and said,

"Petrol."

The man, in shadow, let the bottles drop, took out a single long match, said,

"This is not a safety match."

The old guard, frightened beyond belief, tried,

"What?"

The man, in a quiet reasonable tone, explained,

"It means you can strike it off a piece of wood."

Paused.

Flicked the match against a beam,

Continued (with a hint of amusement),

"It should light instantly."

But it didn't.

The man shrugged, said,

"Nothing's reliable, eh?"

Then asked,

"What's your name?"

The man, scared shitless, managed,

"Sean."

The man nodded as if this was of some import, asked,

"Would you describe yourself as lucky?"

Sean, despite his fear, snarled,

"Yeah, right, lucky, that's me, my fucking cup overflowed."

The man actually *tut-tutted*, reprimanded,

"Now no need for that language. Let's keep a civil tone."

He raised the match, asked,

"What do you say, Sean, want to go again?"

Where questions of

Religion
Are concerned,
People are guilty
Of every possible
Sort of dishonesty
And
Intellectual misdemeanor.

(Freud)

Father Malachy, in waiting to assume the title bishop of Galway, was summoned to the archdiocese.

He got there to find all ranks of clergy from the county assembled.

The good, the bad, and the disgruntled.

There was only one item on the agenda.

The Miracle.

The archbishop, a frail eighty-year-old, called for silence as the milieu had availed its gathering of the decanters of port.

Back in the day, every spirit with a good label had been provided but frugality was now to be seen, if not actually practiced.

Indeed, one parish priest from a tiny parish remarked,

"Even the Holy Spirit is in short supply."

Malachy looked at him, considered him a small fish so didn't bother answering him. Malachy needed to be with the power brokers as questions had been raised recently as to his suitability for bishop.

Malachy had snarled to his wingman Pat

"Suitability? As if there was ever a suitable bishop."

Pat, young, ambitious, nervous, nodded noncommittally.

If Malachy was on the skids, he would need a new patron.

The archbishop spoke.

"Rome is concerned about this recent *event*"—nobody was mentioning the actual "m" word—"and with that foremost in mind, they have very kindly sent us their top investigator."

He moved aside to allow a priest to join him, said,

"This is Monsignor Rael."

A slight ripple ran through the crowd. Tales of this guy were legion and none, none of them augured well.

Heads rolled when Rael arrived.

He was tall, thin, with sallow skin, pockmarked, which for some odd reason summoned up visions of the Mafia.

His eyes were the coldest gray you'd see outside of Galway granite.

He stared at the assembled clergy, said,

"The malignancy of miracles."

The chill of the term hovered over the crowd.

Pat had thought a miracle was a good thing.

Wasn't it?

He added,

"David Hume."

Paused.

Then with a supercilious tone continued,

"No doubt you are all familiar with his work. He said,

I'll believe anything if

You show me the evidence."

Rael leaned forward, shouted,

"But

> *The difficulty with miracles is*
>> *Deciding between the likelihood*
>> *That they have occurred*
>> *And the veracity*
>> *Of the report of them.*"

He scanned the room, settled on the nervous shuffling Pat, commanded,

"You, yes you, what do I mean by that final part."

Pat looked around for help but all eyes were averted. Rael pushed,

"Speak up, man."

Pat, in utter candor, blurted,

"I haven't a frigging clue."

The crowd loved it.

Rael?

Not so much.

He said,

"And that is the future of the Church, God help us all."

Dismissing Pat with a withering look, he said,

"The children, it dies or flies with them."

He let the ominous tone of that linger, then said,

"If this were genuine"—his face suggesting the utter implausibility of such—"the Church could gain a massive boost. We might even have another . . .

Lourdes.

Fatima.

Or even

Medjugorje."

He paused on the third one, the gold mine it had provided in terms of faith, converts, and, best of all, merchandise, like a rock concert that kept on giving, a spiritual Woodstock.

But

They knew the alternative.

"If it's a stunt, we need to stop it now."

Many wondered how you stopped a YouTube sensation.

As if reading their very thoughts, Rael added,

"The Lord works in mysterious ways."

Malachy felt that was as solid a threat as he'd ever heard.

If he'd had another drink in him, he might have voiced,

"Suffer the children."

Because one thing was certain: suffer those little bastards would, one way or another.

Rael dispersed them with various instructions as to finding the children, stifling the media, exploring any advantage available, and reporting back to him. He would be in residence at a house on the bishop's grounds.

Malachy groaned. This meant the blackguard would be literally on his case.

Pat watched as the various clergy went their separate subdued ways. He was keen to learn all the ecclesial terminology, asked Malachy,

"Was that like a synod?"

Malachy, back smoking since the miracle, snapped,

"No, that's what we call a clusterfuck."

Mine is the most peaceable disposition
My wishes are a humble dwelling with a thatched roof

Good bed, good food, milk of the freshest, flowers at my windows
Some fine tall pines before my door

And if the good Lord wants me completely happy
He will grant me the joy

Of seeing some six or seven of my enemies
Hanging from those trees.

(Heine, Heinrich, *Gedanken und Einfäille*)

Living in the country.

And even had the obligatory wax jacket.

Of all the side roads I'd taken, and diverse and maniac they were, the countryside never, never featured.

The only remnant of my past life was a gold miraculous medal, had belonged to my dead daughter.

But I can't dwell on that now, phew-oh.

I'm a city rat.

Born and bred to alleys, backstreets, murky pubs, shady people, coasting slightly above actual poverty and squalor, but always more than comfortable in the noise and rush of a city.

Truth to tell, it was only part time but, still, a major shake-up of my existence. My previous case could be summarized as the *summer of the dead girls*.

Galway dead girls.

And a falcon.

In the midst of horrendous violence and killings, I had saved a badly injured falcon, which led me to a falconer named Keefer.

He was formerly a roadie for the Rolling Stones, had a farm outside town, and was as eccentric/crazy a character as I'd ever met.

We bonded over revenge, a kind of frontier vengeance.

After the smoke had cleared and bodies were buried, I found I'd developed a taste for country air and flying the falcon. It made me feel something I'd not felt for years: alive.

And Keefer.

He was the kind of friend to cherish if you had the dark demons such as I did.

His past appeared to be as troubled and ferocious as mine.

Added bonus, he grew weed and kept a stock of bourbon that would see us through a siege. Without ever actually agreeing to it, we'd come to a tenacious arrangement.

I spent weekends at his farm; he came to town if he felt the urge for society.

He rarely felt sociable, said,

"You tour for twenty years with the Stones, you lose any illusions about people."

I was having coffee in Keefer's cabin when he strode in, carrying neatly chopped wood, sweat running down his Jerry Garcia T-shirt. He was of burly build, with a face you might have called ruined save for the sheer vivacity in his eyes. He was dressed in faded jeans, work boots, and was wiping his face with a Willie Nelson bandanna.

Knowing some of the life he'd led, I wouldn't be surprised if Willie had *actually* given it to him. He poured coffee, lit a joint, sighed, said,

"Hits the spot."

The falcon was in the corner, hooded and making contented sounds. I was learning to distinguish her vocabulary. Keefer listened, then said,

"There's been an offer to buy Maeve."

I'd named her after a nun, a loved wonderful friend who died on my watch.

I asked,

"How much?"

"Three grand."

As Keefer did most of the bird's care, I went,

"Up to you."

He laughed, said,

"Not a fucking chance."

I was well pleased.

I stood up, said,

"I have to head for town, see to my apartment."

He nodded, said,

"Take the jeep, make a statement."

I gave him a look, asked,

"What would that be?"

He thought about it, then,

"Bite me."

State of the nation:

A hundred thousand patients were on trolleys/chairs in hospitals all over the country. The minister for health said, maybe borrowing from *Game of Thrones*,

"Winter is coming."

Brexit continued to limp on, every day bringing new terms to the vocabulary.

> *Backstop.*
> *Soft border.*
> *Hard border.*

The Irish rugby team defeated the All Blacks at the Aviva.

Mick McCarthy took over management of the Irish soccer team.

A small soccer club in Dublin had a fixture postponed due to the death of its star Spanish player; clubs nationwide wore black armbands, tributes poured in.

Two days later the Spanish player was alive and well, working in Galway.

The Blasphemy Act was repealed and, yes, that does sound as surreal as it is.

I parked off Eyre Square, and as I moved away, a car parking guy came running, demanding,

"How long do you intend to remain there?"

He was that lover-of-uniform type, a peaked official cap pulled at what he deemed a menacing angle. He was right up in my face. I asked,

"Is that a metaphysical question as in 'on this earth', or simply a can't-mind-your-own-fucking-business one?"

Rocked him, but he rallied, said,

"You can't talk to me like that."

I gave him my best smile, said,

"I just did."

He pulled out a notebook, the last refuge of the inadequate, said,

"I'll report you."

I looked at him, then wearied of the farce, said,

"Trust me, no one cares, no one."

I went into Garavan's and, thank Christ, nothing had changed. The barman said,

"Been a while."

I nodded, ordered a pint and Jay, went into the snug. Was on the best side of both when a tall distinguished man entered. I say *distinguished* as he was wearing what used to be described as a frock coat, like a gunslinger, had a gleaming white shirt, red tie, and a mop of expensively groomed gray hair. He was in his fifties with narrow mean eyes.

He sat opposite me, declared,

"I am Benjamin J. Cullen."

What was there to say? So I said nothing.

Didn't faze him. He reached in his jacket, produced a long match with a red sulfur top, said,

"This is not a safety match."

I said,

"Fascinating."

This amused him. He said,

"I have followed your colorful exploits down the years and, no offense, but I think you have been fortunate rather than deductive."

I thought that was mildly amusing, so went,

"Better lucky than smart."

He was shaking his head, said,

"Oh, I don't underestimate your, how should I put it . . ."

Pause.

"Sheer tenacity."

I thought there were worse things and asked,

"Is all this meandering eventually going to reach a conclusion?"

He seemed to be weighing this, then said,

"Supposedly a miracle has occurred in our lovely city and I don't want that sideshow to detract from the main event."

His tone was completely serious, so I said,

"Lemme guess, you're going to be the main attraction with whatever lunatic waves that brings."

A flicker of rage in his eyes but brief. He composed himself, said,

"This is really a courtesy. I don't seriously think of you as an adversary but I felt it was simply a touch of etiquette."

He rolled the match in his fingers then placed it in front of me.

I said,
"I don't want your damn match."
He stood up, fixed his hair, said,
"No, keep it. Believe me, I have a whole lot more."

The
  First
Time
        He
              Hit
        Me

He
  Only
Broke
My
  Nose

        (victim impact statement)

I was on the good side of the drink, the *world isn't so bad* illusion.
Of course, I knew it would fade and I'd be

A broken man in a broken country.

But for now, enjoy.

A woman approached, asked,

"Mr. Taylor?"

Lots of descriptions but *mister*, never.

The booze still clicking, I said in a soft tone,

"Whatever it is, whatever you need help with, I can't, I won't."

Maybe a little harsher than intended.

She was in her early thirties, clothes that were clean but modest, her face with a defeated look—perhaps she'd once been pretty but life had demolished that piece by piece. I'd never like to say a woman was *haggard*.

She was.

She put an envelope on the table, said,

"It's not much."

I took a deep breath but before I could start, she went,

"I can tolerate my husband beating me but now he's at my daughter. She's six."

The words,

"*He's at my daughter*."

Phew, the implications, I really, *really* didn't want to hear this.

I said,

"Shoot him."

Took her by storm, she muttered,

"*Shoot?*"

I needed another drink and fast. I emphasized,

"Kill the fucker. He won't stop. The Guards, if they can be bothered, will issue a *caution* but he won't stop. They never do."

She pushed a thin envelope toward me, said,

"'Tis all the money I have."

Her name was on the envelope, written in a beautiful style, almost Gothic script.

Renee Garvey.

I sighed. The child had nailed me. I said,

"I need only one thing."

She perked up a little, hope rising, asked,

"What?"

"A hurley."

I took a walk round the city, feeling off balance from my sojourn in the country. Bizarrely, I missed the falcon on my arm, the sound as she dived from the heights to hit my arm with that almighty *thud*.

Christ, that felt like life.

In the city, everyone glued to mobile phones, stress etched large, I felt suffocated. I went into Starbucks—shows my state of mind—ordered a double espresso, having run the obstacle course of the barista barraging me with questions, as to

Flavor.

Size, and, worse, asked my name.

Fuck.

I snapped, snarled,

"Look, a plain double espresso. I'm not here to freaking bond with you. Just the coffee and, you know, before Tuesday."

He didn't spit in the cup but he sure looked like he wanted to.

There was a cup for tips and I put the change in there and was he grateful?

Was he fuck?

The chatter of the city was *the miracle*.

I was asked more than once,

"Jack, do you believe in miracles?"

I said,

"Take a wild guess."

Adding to the mystery, if mystery there was, was that the children had disappeared.

I said aloud,

"Not my problem."

Five minutes later I was hit by a truck.

A big one.

The expression

I felt like I was hit by a truck.

Let me tell you, *actually* being hit by a truck is a whole other feeling.

It's a blend of deep shock, terror, ferocious pain, then unconsciousness.

I came to in a hospital bed, not feeling anything save panic and the realization that my daughter's miraculous medal was no longer round my neck. In moments of terror I instinctively reached for it.

A nurse said,

"Don't move, I'll get the doctor."

Don't move!

Was she kidding? I couldn't raise my head, a sound in my mind of crushing metal and grinding gears overridden by utter fear.

What I most wanted to do was scream.

Very, very loudly.

And at length

The doctor arrived, with the inevitable chart—your future, or lack of it.

He said,

"Mr. Taylor."

Then paused, a momentary loss, until

"You're a miracle."

I managed to say,

"Seems to be the season for them."

He asked,

"What do you remember?"

"That Mourinho was sacked from Man United."

He gave me a thorough examination with many

Uh-huts, mms, bumphs,

The kind of noises that scare the shite out of you, that imply,

"You're fucked."

He stood back, looked out at me over his glasses, said,

"It's baffling, you were hit full on by a massive truck. Though you've been unconscious for weeks, basically, there's not a scratch on you."

I had no reply to this; I was simply astounded.

I said,

"My miraculous medal is gone."

He added with the hint of a smile,

"No wonder they're calling you *the first miracle of the memorial.*"

Oh, shit, no, no.

I croaked,

"Calling me what?"

He seemed perplexed at my ignorance, said,

"The famine memorial, where the children saw the lady of light. You're the first miracle. It's all over the media: you're a bona fide event."

This was insane. I tried to sit up, near screamed, but my throat hurt, managed,

"The memorial, what in God's name has that to do with a truck blindsiding me?"

He was now concerned, got some water, and handed it to me with two pills, said,

"Easy, you need to stay calm. Take these, they'll help."

Me, I'll always take the pills but I continued to stare at him, waiting for the explanation.

He sighed, said,

"The children, the ones from the memorial that they've been searching for, they tended to you, waited with you until first responders came, then they . . ."

He clicked his fingers,

"Vanished."

He left me to ponder and, fuck, pondering was no help.

A nurse stuck her head round the door, said,

"You up for another visitor?"

I echoed,

"Another?"

She gave that Galway girl smile, part devilment, pure attitude, said,

"We've had to fight off your public."

Saw my face, said quickly,

"I'll get the visitor."

While I awaited the visitor I noticed a ton of flowers, cards, and, uh-huh,

Rosary beads, relics of many saints, even the glove of Padre Pio. Phew-oh.

Alongside this bounty of well wishes was a long black box, like you would find enclosing a fountain pen, tied with a bright red ribbon.

I felt a shiver, recalling Truman Capote's sinister story in *Music for Chameleons*.

Titled "Handcarved Coffins."

Fuck. I shook my head, enough with the dread. I was, after all, a bona fide miracle. What could harm me?

Even without my daughter's medal.

Right?

Opened it and took out a long single match, with a note.

I read,

Jack

Don't panic, it's a safety match.

Think of the painter L. S. Lowry.

You and I are angels in fire.

Think Rilke, a favorite of yours if Google is to be believed, and his line,

"Each angel is terrible."

We will set the city alight.

I am the match, you are the sulfur.

It seems awesomely fitting; you are currently the miracle man,

I am the matchstick man.

Together we will engulf them all.

   Yours in flames,

   B.

A woman appeared in the doorway, a nun?

My heart jumped.

Maeve?

Impossible.

For years, one of my odd friendships had been with Sister Maeve, a lovely, warmhearted soul, who had been literally torn to pieces by two knife-wielding psychos who killed her as part of a vendetta against me.

Both were buried deep, the bad fuckers.

I named the falcon Maeve in her memory.

The woman before me was only kind of a nun.

In her appearance: She had a discreet nun's headgear owing more to Gucci than to the Lord, navy tunic with stylish navy pants, white silk shirt with a hint of red at the collar.

Mostly, she had the rugged blonde hair of a California divorcée and the complexion that spoke of serious cash in its care, her age thus anywhere from forty-five to fifty-eight.

Too, even before she spoke, she radiated that fantastic energy and charisma that people from that state exude. They might not have invented vitamin D but they were a walking testament to the benefit of it.

She said,

"Jack, oh, Jack Taylor."

Yup, definitely American but a British undertone that suggested a Swiss finishing school. She uttered my name in a tone that was rare in my experience. Usually, someone said my name, chaos lurked behind.

But this, this was delight tinged with a type of wonder.

Fuck, I felt better already.

Then—I know this sounds highly unlikely—she blushed. Certainly a red hue appeared in her healthy face. She gasped,

"Where are my manners? I'm Sister Consuela of the Sisters of Solace, but most people call me Connie."

I echoed,

"Like S.O.S."

She didn't get it, looked askance, so I said,

"Like the emergency code."

Then she got it and smiled in delight, said,

"Oh, I heard you were whip smart, sharp as a scalpel."

I was still holding the match and she looked at it, in question mode, so I asked,

"Do you smoke?"

Idiotic question. Finding a Californian who smoked would be like finding a priest who wasn't nervous in the present climate of scandals.

She said,

"No, but I used to."

Then tittered, I mean actually tittered, as if she'd escaped from a chick-lit scene, admitted,

"In my wild days, oh sweet Lord, I was a rock chick."

Keefer would be a match (no pun much intended) for her.
I asked,

"What kind of nun are you? I mean, what order: Carmelites,
Poor Clares, you get the gist."

This both amused and vaguely embarrassed her. She said,

"Hmm, my husband left me for the ubiquitous younger
model, and a bunch of gal pals and I used to meet regularly
to read scripture and"—giggled a little—"okay, some of Fifty
Shades of Whatever. Due to a series of blessed events we decided
to become nuns but not with any formal rules or obedience to
some old bitch who was bitter and frigid."

A nice edge of hard leaked over the last part and she got me
even more interested. I said,

"Rebels without a veil."

She said, with a tiny hint of offense,

"We take our calling very seriously."

I had managed to sit up, even sip some water, said,

"Like L. Ron Hubbard."

Now she did snarl.

"We are nothing like Scientology."

I gave a tight smile, no relation to humor, said,

"You have a problem with your comprehension, much like
any church, really. What I meant was the saying by him, *If you
want to make a million, found a religion*."

Before she could answer, I asked,

"Do you pay taxes?"

A moment before she answered, then,

"I didn't come here to discuss financial issues."

I laughed, said,

"That would be a no: No, you don't pay taxes so, tell me, why did you come?"

She was well rattled but took a moment to compose herself, then the cheery Californian resumed.

"We had been looking at Ireland as a base for our sisterhood and then we heard of the miracle, looked up Galway, and just knew it was divine providence."

I had no reply to this nonsense so said nothing.

She was on a roll so continued, said,

"The miracle of Jack Taylor. It is perfect. A former lost soul, an alcoholic, a drug addict, prone to extreme violence, the cause of grief to so many, and God chose you, the most wretched of his creatures, to bestow his grace upon."

Fuck.

I said,

"Flattery won't work on me."

She looked at me with that blend of pity and condescension that pharmacists reserve for some poor bastard who tries to buy meds with codeine in them.

She said,

"We've set up our convent near the shrine of the memorial and already hundreds of people are camping out there. Imagine what your appearance would mean."

I was choking with rage, tried,

"What is it exactly you think I am supposed to do?"

She got that look of bliss that fundamentalists have when they are at their craziest, said,

"Saint Jack, that's what they're calling you. We can make Galway a city of global pilgrimage."

The nurse came in. Trish, I think she was called. I told her,

"This woman thinks I'm a saint."

Trish suppressed a burst of laughter, said,

"She should try nursing you."

Connie rounded on her, spittle at the corner of her fading botoxed lips, near spat,

"Respect please: This is a man of deep spirituality."

Trish gave her a long look, said,

"You need your head examined."

Then turned to me, said,

"There's some kind of Hells Angel being held by security. He claims to live with you."

Keefer.

Exactly what this shindig needed.

I said,

"Let him in."

He arrived looking like a cross between a biker and an outlaw, his hair in a ponytail, that Willie Nelson bandanna, leather jacket with a denim vest over it, combat pants, motorcycle boots, a battered rucksack on his shoulder. He stood, exclaimed,

"Taylor, you're back."

He nodded at Connie, noncommittal, who just gaped, said to her,

"Be a good gal, shut the door."

She didn't like it, echoed,

"I beg your pardon?"

He smiled, said,

"It's not complicated: Shut the bloody door, on your way out, preferably."

He plonked the rucksack on the bed, took out a bottle of Old Grand-Dad, two mugs, poured liberally, handed me one, said,

"Stay away from Mack trucks, buddy."

Connie was horrified, shrieked,

"What if a doctor comes by?"

He looked at her as if she were a simpleton, said,

"Why I asked you to shut the door."

Then adding heresy to blasphemy, he lit up a joint, drew deep, handed it to me. I was in heaven, reeling from the hit of neat booze, the rawness of the joint.

Connie near screamed,

"Do you know who I am?"

Indignation writ huge.

He shrugged.

"Sure, the broad running the Sisters of Something scam."

She turned to me, said,

"Say something."

I raised the mug, tried,

"*Sláinte.*"

Connie considered her options, which were few, decided on flight, said,

"I shall withdraw for now. But Jack, we'll be seeing each other: We have important work to do."

Then to Keefer,

"The Sisters of Solace will not be mocked."

And she was gone.

Keefer said,

"I could be wrong but I think she took a bit of a shine to me."

Then he added,

"Reminds me of Joan Didion, who was described as having *cool bitch chic.*"

I said,

"You'd make quite the pair."

He laughed, then,

"You missed Christmas."

I nodded gravely as if some losses must just be endured.

Asked,

"How is our falcon?"

His face shone, he said,

"She hunts like a thing of beauty."

I showed him the match and the note from the matchstick man. He read it with a worried frown, said,

"We'll have to find this lunatic."

I said,

"Not too hard. Let's see how many fires there've been."

That hatred is a system that, however much it may be held in check by other forces of character, works for the destruction of the hated thing, as anger does only in its extreme forms, and in human beings works with a deliberate and self-controlled activity as one of its distinctive marks, is generally recognized.

Destruction then becomes the prominent end of hatred.

All means may be adopted for this end.

(Rvnd. Alexander F. Shand)

Benjamin J. Cullen.

A fine worthy name he felt.

Nobody called him

Benny

Or Ben

Or any of those mundane derivations.

At least they never called him that a second time.

He was in his late forties. His looks were average, nothing stood out. He liked it thus and dressed accordingly, conservative but expensive.

He was fueled by hate.

A dark, uncompromising, all-encompassing hatred, and he hugged it to himself like a malevolent lover. He didn't have a tortured childhood; like everything else, it was mundane. Ordinary parents who were too normal to detect anything amiss in their only son. He was quiet, which suited their quiet dispositions.

In his late teens he had discovered *The Art of War*

By Sun Tzu.

It spoke to him directly when he memorized chapter 12.

"The Attack by Fire."

Which began,

There are five ways of attacking with fire. The first is to burn soldiers in their camp; the second is to burn stores; the third is to burn trains; the fourth is to burn magazines arsenals; the fifth is to hurl dropping fire amongst the enemy.

He would adapt this thesis to suit himself like all the best nutjobs. He was chuffed to learn that Tony Soprano quoted the book in the television series. Later it amused him to learn that the two most read books in American prisons were

> *The Art of War*

And

> Sidney Sheldon, *The Other Side of Midnight*.

He'd never admit it, his arrogance and intellectual contempt would not allow it, but he did once sneak a peek at the Sheldon, muttered,

"A precursor to the era of Kardashians."

His mantra was simple:

Burn everything.

What did burn was his intelligence. And with it rode contempt. He learned early to adopt a facade of acceptance so he could blend in.

He was fascinated by the concept of *love*.

He heard mutterings,

I love you

Love to

Love always

And was truly baffled.

Now hate, it felt real, set you afire, and even the very expression

I hate you

Shocked in its simplicity.

He had a twisted sense of the absurd, liked to say,

"*Ah, love, what's not to hate?*"

His favorite expression, the one that really got him, was

"*I love you to death.*"

Ah, bliss.

He could nearly grasp it.

Nearly.

He'd studied to become an accountant. Figures were feelings-free, no emotion attached. Then he met Alison. She was no beauty but she gave him camouflage, until,

Until,

She said, after a few short weeks,

"We're done."

Instant rage, brimming under a tight icy politeness as he asked,

"Why?"

She smoked the odd cigarette, especially when she was nervous, and had the habit of using long matches, as if she had to keep the flame at a distance.

She said,

"You don't set me alight."

Three weeks later, the dorm she lived in was burned to the ground. Alison and two other girls didn't survive.

Benjamin bought a box of long matches after the funerals.

Nonsafety brand.

There was once in the country of Alifay.
A sad city.
The saddest of cities.
A city so ruinously sad.
It had forgotten its name.

(Salman Rushdie, *Haroun and the Sea of Stories*)

I was finally leaving the hospital. All the tests had been done and the doctor continued to express his astonishment.

He advised me to

Take things easy.

I looked at him, asked,

"You ever hear of the singer Iris DeMent?"

He hadn't.

I said,

"She has a song that says, *easy's gettin' harder every day.*"

He considered that, said,

"I actually think I understand."

The nurse looked in, said,

"There's a priest here to see you."

Even the doctor smiled as I said,

"Tell him he's too late, I didn't die."

Malachy burst into the room, looking tired, irritable, and very unholy.

He accused,

"You're all right?"

The doctor wisely slipped away. I said,

"Sorry to disappoint."

He was genuinely puzzled, went,

"But a Mack truck hit you."

I asked,

"You haven't heard about my miracle?"

Not impressed, he said,

"The luck of the very devil."

I asked,

"Are you the bishop yet?"

He looked like a child whose toy has been stolen, said,

"They're going with some other bollix."

I tried not to smile, said,

"Least you've accepted the decision with grace."

He didn't seem to hear, said,

"I wanted that gig."

Then, snapping back to his usual surliness, said,

"They've sent a hatchet guy from Rome."

Now I was amused, asked,

"To silence you?"

He stared at me, said,

"The reason I'm here, I was sent to arrange a meeting with him for you."

"No,"

I said.

He was kind of delighted but said,

"He's from Rome."

I said,

"Look at me. Do I look like I give a fuck."

He was seriously glad, offered,

"They don't take no as an answer, it's not Church policy."

In there was a hint of fear. I said,

"If they make you bishop, I'll maybe meet him."

He stood for a moment, said,

"This is the first time I think I've ever liked you."

My apartment had that forlorn look that a place gets when no one has been there for months.

It had the look of a sad place in a sad city at a sad time.

I had brought the essentials on my way.

Bottle of Jay.

Twelve-pack.

I opened all the windows, let the wind of Galway Bay shoo out the bad memories, though it would need to be a ferocious one to accomplish that.

My body was weak from six weeks in hospital so I'd resolved on fierce long walks to rebuild. I looked round and the whole atmosphere was forlorn, a fitting epithet for my life. I shook myself, made a strong black coffee, added a hint of Jay, muttered,

"Get a grip."

In a moment of industry I sat down, dealt with the bills, and even had some money left when they were done. The one thing I had always held on to, my Garda all-weather coat, had been left at the home of Maeve the nun, only a few hours before she was murdered.

She had given me the gift of a navy wax Barbour coat. It had disappeared after the truck ran me over. I wasn't too sorry, but how could I wear it when it was a constant reminder of Maeve?

There was an old pea jacket I could use for the time being. I put that on over an Aran sweater, a Galway United scarf and watch cap, then headed out to begin my rehabilitation.

The end of January, it was bitter cold but I killed it, walked from the diving boards at Blackrock, along the prom, down Grattan Road.

It was a comfort to have the ocean on my right during the walk: I have always found a deep yearning from the sea, but yearning for what?

Fuck knows.

The locals I met seemed to sing from the same hymn sheet, like this:

"You're alive!"

Or

"You're a miracle."

Halfway along Grattan Road I stopped in utter dismay.

The famine memorial, where the supposed miracle occurred, was surrounded by tents, not just a few scattered around but hundreds, stretching to the Claddagh, like a mini city.

Banners were proclaiming THE MIRACLE OF GALWAY.

I kept my head down and tried to move past quickly but heard shouts of,

"It's him."

Oh, fuck.

People began streaming toward me, wanting to touch me, and I think I heard, I hope to Christ not, "*Heal me.*"

I was going to be crushed by hysterical piety.

A car pulled up, door thrown open, and a voice urging,

"Get in, for fuck's sake."

Owen Daglish, the only remaining friend I had in the Guards. I was barely in when he hit the gas, blew out of there.

He glanced at me, accused,

"You must be out of your mind coming here."

Indeed.

He drove on past the golf club, found a hotel toward Spiddal, turned in, pulled up, said,

"Let's get a drink."

No argument there.

The hotel was quiet; in the bar was a lone female bartender who smiled, said,

"Welcome, gentlemen."

Owen grunted, not accustomed to civility, ordered,

"Two pints, two Jameson chasers."

Looked at me, asked,

"For you?"

I stared at him before he said,

"Jeez, lighten up. I'm kidding."

He handed over a fistful of notes, said to the woman,

59

"We'll be at the corner table. Try not to fuck up the pints."

We sat, in silence, needing the drinks.

When they came, Owen examined the heads of the pints, said,

"Not bad."

I said to the woman.

"Thanks a lot."

The woman moved away. Owen asked,

"The fuck is with you? *Thank you*? You trying to make me look bad?"

I took a sip of the Jay, said,

"No, you need no help there. You manage to bollix all by your lonesome."

He downed the pint in almost one go, burped, said,

"Ah, better."

Then to me,

"This fucking miracle business is some mad shite. Half the city is delighted at the incoming business, the other half is worried about controlling the chaos."

He thought about that, asked,

"You think there was anything in that first event? I mean, you and the truck is just blind luck . . ."

Did I believe there had been miracle/miracles?

No.

I said,

"I think the world is so fucked. Trump has America literally shut down, Brexit is a mess beyond belief, Venezuela is becoming the new Syria in the worst way, so people are desperate for something miraculous. There was never really a better time to provide a miracle."

He ordered another round. I said,

"Not for me. I'm supposed to take it easy."

He laughed, snorted,

"That'll be the day."

Indeed.

He worked on the fresh drinks, then,

"Your name came up in another case."

I said,

"I have the perfect alibi: a coma."

He asked,

"You ever meet . . . wait, I'll check my notes.

Took out a battered Garda notebook. I felt the familiar pang of regret at having been thrown out of the force. He double-checked, then continued.

"Renee Garvey?"

It sort of rang a bell but elusive. I said,

"Why?"

He said,

"She has a young daughter who is obviously a victim of abuse but is in some sort of shock and not talking. The mother, Renee, was apparently thrown through a third-floor window, worse, a closed window."

I asked,

"Did she survive?"

He gave me a withering look, said,

"No miracle for her, she's dead as dirt."

I felt terrible. Now I remembered her desperation and how flippant I had been.

More points on the guilt sheet. I said,

"I failed her."

He looked at me, interested, asked,

"What'd you say to her?"

I could recall the words clearly. I said,

"I told her to get a hurley."

He shook his head, said,

"You're a cold fuck, Taylor."

And he was my friend?

I asked,

"Where is the husband?"

"He has a solid alibi but we're fairly sure it's him. He is one vicious bastard and only last week collected the insurance on her, which he is now drinking big-time."

I asked,

"Where does he hang?"

He shook his head, ordered,

"No, no way, stay out of this."

I tried,

"If only to offer my condolences."

He stood up, said,

"Condolences, like fuck. You can walk back, see it as penance."

I sat there, looking at an empty glass, as empty as my soul.

It was a long walk back to town but the power of the wind, the unaccustomed pints after my hospital sojourn, helped me walk, if not briskly, at least determinedly.

In town, on a whim, I went to the Protestant church, St. Nicholas, seven hundred years old. A man inside the door, guiding visitors, welcomed me. Said his name was Andrew. He had warmth that I no longer felt in my own churches.

Best of all, the candles were not the electronic ones littering my usual churches. Real candles, with a long taper to light them. It was reassuring in the old way. There was no slot for money; that seriously impressed me.

A German couple stopped, asked me,

"Do you know the Crane Bar?"

I did.

A TV series was currently filming there. I gave them directions and they said,

"We love Galway."

What do you say to that? I said,

"And Galway loves you."

We can now repeat
    That all of them are illusions and insusceptible of proof.
    Some of them are so improbable,
    So incompatible with everything we have discovered
about the reality of the world, that we may compare
them—if we pay proper regard to the psychological
differences—to delusions.

                                        (Freud)

The nurses were staging a one-day strike, the government was deep in panic as to what would happen if the U.K. crashed out of the EU with no deal in place. Talk of return to a hard border in the North sent shivers through the land; already, two bombs had been exploded in Derry.

Trump was pictured in the White House surrounded by hundreds of McDonald's Big Macs, fries, milkshakes, for his guests.

A priest refused Communion to a politician who, he said, "Supported abortion."

Another step in the Church's insane determination to alienate all of the people all of the time.

I was in my apartment, reading Declan Coyle's *The Green Platform*. I literally had weights on my feet, doing exercises to strengthen the wasted muscles: The weights on my mind had no known exercise to help there.

There was a timid knock on my door.

All sorts of calls had come in the past and none of them ever could be described as timid; knocks usually announced chaos and strife.

I opened the door cautiously. A woman in her fifties stood there, holding a large parcel. She was dressed in what used to be called *a sensible coat*.

Meaning no frills, simply utilitarian.

She had a face about one feature short of prettiness but energy there suggested a decent nature, which in my troubled life implied she was not going to knife me in the doorway.

Yet.

She had an unlined face, such as you observe only in nuns.

She asked,

"Jack Taylor?"

I nodded: She put out her small hand, said,

"I'm Saoirse, a friend of Sister Maeve."

Phew-oh.

I said,

"Come in."

She sat near the window, the large package near her feet. I asked,

"Tea, coffee, whiskey?"

She gave a lovely smile, tinged with melancholia, said,

"No, thank you."

I asked,

"Are you a nun?"

I seemed to be up to my arse in nuns. She said,

"Heavens, no. Maeve and I have . . ."

Paused, corrected,

"*Had* been friends since school."

Then silence until she shook herself, said,

"Dear me, you must be wondering why I'm here—it's just so odd to meet you after all Maeve told me."

Oops.

I tried,

"I was not always at my best in her company."

Alarm on her face, she protested,

"Oh no, Good Lord, she loved you."

Wallop my heart. I was astonished, went,

"What?"

She gave me a look that showed some steel beneath the gentle face, asked,

"Nuns can't love?"

I was lost, said,

"I'm going to have a drink. You want something?"

She relented, asked,

"Perhaps a small sherry?"

I laughed, said,

"Seriously, I look like a guy who keeps *sherry*?"

I couldn't quite keep the contempt from my tone, and added,

"Sherry is what you drink in Lent, for bloody penance."

She bowed her head, as if I'd punched her. I attempted,

"Um, didn't mean that to sound so harsh."

She gave a tiny smile, said,

"Maeve said you were angry at the world."

I bit down, lest I do more verbal carnage, poured two Jays, left her glass beside her, knocked back my own. She indicated the package at her feet, said,

"That is for you."

When I made no move, she continued,

"Your Garda jacket was at Maeve's. She asked me to put it in the dry cleaners. Said it was the only real link you had to your past, but she . . ."

Pause.

"Died, before she could collect it so I felt I should honor her wish."

I still didn't move, I was so taken aback.

She stood, adjusted her coat, said,

"Well, I'll be going. Thank you for seeing me."

She let herself out the door and was gone.

I have done a lot of shitty things in my life, reached all sorts of lows, but, right then, right there, I felt I had hit a whole new level of bollix.

Sister Consuela/Connie was in a rage, said,

"I'm so angry I could freaking spit."

Her second in command, a woman from New York named Brid, had just told her that the expected revenue from new recruits hadn't materialized.

Their hastily erected tent, close to the site of the miracle, had cost them more cold cash than anticipated. Brid said,

"These Irish muthus, these sons of bitches, they have so much work from other interested parties that they can charge what they like."

And indeed, every half-baked religious band/con men/charities/refugee campaigners were vying for tent space close to the memorial.

Miracles were a surefire chance to make a fast buck but the window was small. Public interest would fade, the media would lose interest, and the golden calf of lucre would be lost.

Connie asked,

"Did you find the children?"

They were key.

Who held the children held the ace.

Brid said,

"I know where they are but, again, 'it costs' for the info."

Connie was scheming like a banshee; she'd survived two marriages to two assholes, served a year in hard-core prison for fraud, and knew how to fight.

Mostly, she knew how to fight dirty.

Ireland was pretty much the last chance for the Sisters of Solace to acquire a presence. Connie allowed herself a rare cigarette, Virginia Slims, blew furious clouds of smoke, asked,

"What is needed to differentiate this miracle from all the other gigs?"

Lourdes

Knock

Medjugorje

Fatima

It was telling that Connie saw all these shrines as *gigs*.

Brid said,

"Well, they usually have poor children, seeing the Madonna, promising reward for penance, and, publicized properly, they create a whole industry."

Connie, not the most patient of nuns, snapped,

"I know all that, but what, what has never happened with them all?"

Brid didn't know, was wishing Connie wouldn't blow smoke in her direction.

Connie said,

"Graham Greene said,

> *Why after all should*
> *We expect God*
> *To punish the innocent*
> *With mere living.*"

Brid didn't know much about Graham Greene and had no idea what the quote meant so she said nothing.

Connie was excited as the notion crystallized in her mind, said,

"For the visionaries to die."

Brid had been with Connie long enough to know she had a deep, well-hidden insanity, a madness that knew very little of morality, but she was appalled as she risked,

"You mean hurt the children?"

Connie's face lit up. She said,

"Exactly. Kill the little bastards."

Meanwhile, Benjamin J. Cullen had selected a new target. He didn't have a system of choice, relying on someone crossing his path who invoked his ire.

Such was Thomas Rooney, an American grad student at National University of Ireland, Galway. This was a cosy racket to lure naive Americans to *study in the West of Ireland.* Hopscotch of

Joyce.

Beckett.

Yeats.

And the usual suspects.

Were put on a reading list for the gullible Yanks, then doled out in haphazard lectures by Real Irish Writers.* The yearlong course cost upwards of 15,000 bucks. Plus of course the grad students would be given the opportunity to drink in real Irish pubs with the above writers and talk shite.

Rooney's path crossed Benjamin's in Garavan's, where Rooney was lecturing a young woman on the merits of Beckett versus Joyce.

---

* Real Irish Writers had three distinctive features: 1. They didn't work. 2. They didn't write. 3. They adored footnotes.

Benjamin had actually interrupted Rooney mid-lecture, said mildly,

"I think you need to reread *Krapp's Last Tape* before you attempt to discourse on his merits."

Rooney had looked at him with derision, dismissed him with,

"What would you know? You're too old to even grasp the meaning of *Godot*."

Benjamin felt the age insult was way out of line. It didn't take more than two days for the insult to mutate to hate.

Rooney had a ground-floor apartment along the canal, had been out for a scatter of pints with a Joyce scholar who had insisted,

"All you need to understand about Joyce is contained in the line *shite and onions*."

Rooney had no idea what that meant but felt it might be the kind of conversational showstopper he could drop among his fellow students.

Took him a few minutes to fumble his key into the lock, finally managed it, staggered into the hallway, and was hit hard on the back of the head.

He came to, tied to his one kitchen chair and his clothes drenched in liquid, a liquid that smelled strongly of . . .

Of what?

Gas?

Diesel?

A man was standing by the door, holding something in his hand, something small; the guy looked vaguely familiar. Rooney stared at him in terror. The man said,

"See this?"

Held up a long single match, continued,

"This is not a safety match so basically it should light against, say, this doorjamb."

He struck the match against the wood, it didn't catch, he said,

"Oops."

He asked,

"What do you say, best of three?"

Not only is this stranger not worthy of love but confess, he has more claim to my hostility, even my hatred.

If it will do him any good, he has no hesitation in injuring me.

If he can merely get a little pleasure out of it, he thinks nothing of jeering at me, insulting me, slandering me, showing his power over me, the more secure he feels himself.

(Freud, on human evil)

During my last case, mourning the death of my child, I'd been truly certifiably insane. One especially dark evening, I'd bundled up all my prized books, wrapped them in a cotton bag, gone down to the beach, and burned them all.

Did clean up the debris.

I'm all for keeping our beaches clean.

Since Keefer and, of course, the falcon, I'd been slowly rebuilding my library.

A few trips to Charlie Byrne's, lively chat with Vinny and Noirin, and my bookshelf was beginning to look less sparse.

But haphazard.

My sanity was still very much in the neighborhood of unstable.

I think the selection of books I had well reflected not so much my dilettante taste as my fragile sense of identity.

Like this:

American Rhapsody by Joe Eszterhas.

Shovel Ready by Adam Sternbergh.

Kill by Anthony Good.

Can You Ever Forgive Me? by Lee Israel.

You'd be hard pressed to find a greater range that included utter madness to sublime writing, plus of course two of them contained shades of darkness that I understood absolutely.

I rarely read dystopian fiction, feeling the world was spinning enough out of control without needing a postapocalyptic narrative, but one book, *The Last* by Hanna Jameson, was so utterly special I read it twice.

Mid book musings, a knock at the door. I half expected Keefer but, no, a thin man, dressed in a dark suit, hatchet face, either an ill assassin or a poor undertaker. He asked,

"Jack Taylor?"

A tone of command.

Do first impressions really matter? I don't know but I disliked this guy instantly. I asked,

"What do you want?"

He assessed me, saw nothing that impressed him, asked,

"May I come in? I won't take up much time and I will pay for your valuable time."

He let a drop of disdain drip from *valuable*.

Mildly interested, I let him in; he surveyed the apartment in all its bare essentials, stood by the window, hands clasped behind his back, like a school principal, said,

"I'm Monsignor Rael."

When I made no reply to this, he continued,

"I understand you have been of some small service to Mother Church in the past and we would like to engage your specialist talent once more."

I said,

"My service was more an accident than design."

He smiled, not a pretty sight. He had good teeth but the action gave him an even more skeletal appearance. He said,

"I admire modesty, which shows me you are indeed the man for our small mission."

I took a guess, said,

"If it's about the miracle, either you want the kids or you want them to shut the fuck up."

He was surprised and then moved his hands to give me a brief applause, said,

"I was informed that you are shrewder than you let on."

He reached in his jacket, took out a thick envelope, laid it on the table, said,

"This should cover any expenses you incur."

I asked,

"If, and it's a big *if*, I find the children, what am I supposed to do, give you a bell?"

He laid a business card beside the envelope, said,

"Yes, call that number and we'll take good care of them."

I looked right into his face, asked,

"Hand over children to the Church. Isn't that the shite you guys have been covering up for decades?"

He shook his head, spoke slowly, as if to be fully understood,

"The Church does not wish a miracle at this time."

It was too arrogant to even anger me. I said,

"Best be on your way, pal."

Didn't faze him. He reached for the door, said,

"I'll expect your call."

I said,

"It is truly staggering. You lot have learned nothing, absolutely nothing, from all the bad press."

A final smile as he said,

"Trust me, Taylor, we have learned more than you could imagine: We have learned who to buy."

After he'd gone, I realized he left the envelope. I asked myself,

"Does he think I'm bought?"

For the first in a long time, I smiled, muttered,

"What you've bought is so far from what you think you paid for."

I heard about the arson on the news. Jimmy Norman, in his weekly video show/podcast, wondered aloud if this fire was connected to the previous fire in the warehouse. I now had three problems.

The guy who left me the long match. Was he the arsonist, and why was he contacting me?

The woman who'd come to me for help with her abusive husband. She was now dead and the husband had a solid alibi.

The children of the miracle. Where were they and how would I find them?

Keefer was in town and I was treating him to a pint in Garavan's. He looked more than ever like a Hells Angel. The barman eyed him suspiciously. I said,

"It's okay. He's with me."

The barman said,

"Why is that not in the least bit reassuring?"

I raised my pint, toasted,

"*Sláinte*."

To Keefer.

Who answered,

"Paint it black."

Indeed.

He told me that Maeve, our falcon, was flying strong and proud and I realized how much I missed the sheer joy of seeing her soar. I said,

"I have three problems."

He finished his pint, said,

"Spill."

I did.

He asked,

"How the fuck did you get your own self in the middle of this clusterfuck?"

I had wondered that same dilemma my whole career. He said,

"No biggie. We divide and find solutions."

I had the envelope from the monsignor, took out the fat wad of money, split it in half, handed one to Keefer. He was bemused, asked,

"You're putting me on payroll?"

I said,

"The Church gave me that."

He whistled, said,

"Sweet."

We headed out in search of, if not justice, at least retaliation. I figured if the children had been in the refugee camp in the Claddagh, and that was but a short prayer from the miracle memorial, I'd start there.

Turned out the woman in charge of the refugee center was known to me. She'd been married to a Guard I'd known and I had helped her out in some distant past. I asked her,

"How did two Hispanic children end up here?"

She was in her forties, a no-nonsense type, who'd seen the worst of humanity and didn't expect that to improve anytime soon. She said,

"A fuck-up. The kids were swept up in Trump's first roundup of the migrant columns from South America, then some bright spark allocated them on a ship bound for Europe as the Europeans were still a little tolerant. The kids ended up in the horrendous camps on Greek islands among the Syrian people. An Irish charity literally came in the night, took as many children as they could, and made it to the coast of Ireland."

She seemed exhausted by the story.

I asked,

"And now, do you know where they are?"

She studied me, said,

"I do."

I tried,

"Might you tell me?"

"No."

I tried,

"Listen, those kids tended to me when I was hit by the truck. The very least I can do is thank them."

Sincerity is not my best asset but I felt I managed it quite well.

She stared at me in disbelief.

I asked,

"What, I can't be grateful?"

She shook her head in dismissal, said,

"Of all the things I've heard about you, naivete was never one of them."

I was lost, asked,

"What do you mean?"

She was really dismayed, asked,

"You really don't get it?"

Anger in my tone now, I pushed,

"Get what?"

She said very quietly,

"They weren't helping you, Jack."

When I didn't answer, she said,

"They were trying to rob you."

Keefer found the arsonist, or rather the arsonist found him. Keefer had done the round of pubs, dives, picking up bits and pieces but nothing solid and, down by the docks, he sat on the quay, rolled a smoke, heard,

"You are Mr. Taylor's wingman?"

Turned to see a fairly nondescript man in a gray suit who said,

"I'm Benjamin J. Cullen."

Keefer eyed him slowly, asked,

"You the dude who likes long nonsafety matches?"

Benjamin said,

"A question with a question, how terrifically Irish."

Before Keefer could reply, Benjamin continued,

"But like my good self you are not Irish. Your heritage is somewhat muddled but you, I believe, did some long servitude with a rock and roll band."

Keefer was slightly amused, did half admire the cojones of the guy, answered,

"*The* rock and roll band, the Rolling Stones."

Benjamin made a mock bow, said,

"My apologies but the vagaries of such a genre are not my strong point."

The element of mockery rode point on his tone: Keefer let that stew before he answered,

"But burning people, that's more your line."

Benjamin moved a foot closer, not quite a threat but not without a certain menace. He said,

"A perilous allegation and, alas, not a shred of evidence."

Keefer stood, did a long flex of his back muscles, asked,

"What makes you think I'm the type who ever cared about proof?"

Almost sleight of hand, Benjamin produced a long match, said,

"A token of my esteem."

Keefer took it, snapped it, flicked it to the water, said,

"We'll bury you in the country, with the other crazies."

Turned on his heel, hummed as he strolled away.

If Benjamin was a fait with the Stones, he might have recognized "Sweet Virginia."

Benjamin shouted,

"There was no need to toss the match, let alone break it. I mean, that was just . . ."

He struggled for the word to describe the action, settled for the lame

"Mean!"

Keefer laughed.

In his world, *mean* was just about the most basic tool for survival; he took it as the height of flattery. It was a few hours yet until he met up with Jack, so he decided to take a pit stop. Headed for O'Neachtain's, the kind of pub on Quay Street where his appearance wouldn't cause any waves.

It was packed, guys who looked like they were *something in the arts*. What exactly that might be, even they hadn't quite figured.

And the women.

Ah.

They looked like they'd come right off the stage of one of Synge's plays, all shawls and wringing hands. The smell of hash lingered on the air and that of course made Keefer right at home. He ordered a pint, settled back to watch it being poured.

Done right, the drawing of a Guinness is a work of art, and the longer the better. He rested his boot along the stool beside him, leaned on the bar, feeling comfortable.

The bar guy put the pint before him, asked,

"Anything else?"

Keefer surveyed the pint in admiration, said,

"Maybe a shot of bourbon."

Got that.

Keefer offered,

"Something for yourself?"

The bar guy gave a wide grin, said,

"No, thank you. Are you a Yank?"

Keefer said no but asked,

"You hear tell of a dude named Garvey?"

Before the guy could say the city had a whole shelf of Garvey, Keefer added,

"He lost his wife tragically some time back."

Something changed in what had been a friendly dynamic. The guy physically moved back, his eyes flicked over to a man nursing a pint in the corner, then back to Keefer. He said,

"Can't help you there."

Keefer let some time linger, then walked over to Garvey. Everything about the man spelled hostility. He was tall but stooped, a face like a wet rag, hair that needed a wash, and a track suit that had never known detergent. He looked at Keefer with malice, asked,

"Something bothering you?"

Aggression spilled all over his tone. He had his now empty glass clenched in his left hand. Keefer had encountered the type in many after-gig parties, the type who, as the term went, *glassed you*. Of the many varieties of violence Keefer had witnessed, a glass in the face he rated as the very pit of cowardice.

Keefer leaned back on his boots, said,

"I bet you a hundred bucks I can shove that glass up your ass before you can move it."

Garvey's face went through a permutation of decisions, most involving damage, but in his feral mind something told him, *don't*.

He went with,

"The fuck are you?"

Keefer shot out a hand, letting it rest lightly on Garvey's shoulder, said,

"I'm the guy who hates dudes that beat on women."

Garvey tried,

"There's no proof, nothing. I had an alibi when the bitch died."

Realizing he'd spat *bitch*, he went,

"I mean . . ."

Trailed off.

Keefer gave him a final tap on the shoulder, said,

"Karma, now that's a bitch."

Nodded to the bar guy as he left.

Keefer stood on Quay Street, watching the various buskers, con artists, tourists, and muttered,

"To think I left the countryside for this."

A man stepped up to him, offered a T-shirt with the logo

> *All in all*
> *I'm just another*
> *Prick*
> *With a wall*

Keefer said,

"Pink Floyd okay with you nicking their lyrics? Those bands, they're precious about copyright."

The guy stared at him, asked,

"Who's Pink Floyd?"

Keefer thought,

The world is more fucked than I thought.

Sister Consuela/Connie was about to pack it in. She hadn't been able to locate the miracle children, and the projected increase in followers to her sisterhood not only had not increased but the few she did have had legged it.

She'd had huge hopes for her brand of religion; it glorified freedom and a certain laxity that should have been a draw.

No.

Didn't happen.

She said aloud,

"Fuck."

Her second in command, though precious little to actually command anymore, asked,

"So what now?"

Indeed.

For maybe the first time in her varied career, Connie was all out of ideas. She had been, among other things, a therapist (being Californian, it was near mandatory), a prison chaplain (how she'd recruited Brid, doing a jolt for assault), a real estate gal (the territory of divorcées who'd been shafted), and a financial adviser (which led to her near indictment), but in her mind she had never, never for fuck sakes, been a failure. So she'd skirted real close to the legal wind but was never out of schemes or self-belief.

With icy bitterness, she said,

"I need a blasted miracle."

In the twisted way of the Irish universe, at that moment a man arrived and, if far from being miraculous, he was certainly out of the ordinary. He stood before the two semi-nuns, declared,

"I am Benjamin J. Cullen."

* * *

Brid.

Brid was fucked by nurture and nature.

Coming out of Compton in the worst years of that doomed suburb, she was lost from the get-go. She was doing a jolt in the toughest prison in California when she heard of the *golden chaplain*.

Sister Consuela was the patron saint of inmates. It was rumored she supplied not only the hackneyed solace but pills, the most valuable commodity in jail. Too, she knew how to game the system. Brid was highly cynical before she met her, not believing the hype until . . .

Until

She met her.

And was smitten, utterly.

Here came the symbol of the California dream babe, tall, blonde, confident, and, best of all, sassy. When she walked into Brid's cell, Brid had a shank ready, prepared to gut the bitch, but, instead, this vision moved straight to her, laid a tanned hand on her head, whispered,

"Be still."

And she was.

The nun asked her,

"How would you like to be my wingbird?"

Whatever.

She'd be whatever was asked.

On her release, she went to work straightaway for Connie and now, many failed ventures later, they were in the West of Ireland.

Brid liked to drink, to drink a lot, and then she was prone to talk. Of the many features in Brid that Connie had curbed and changed, the booze was not among them. Plus, it did have an upside.

For Connie.

When dark shit had to be done, and God knows, with Connie's checkered past, a lot of dark deeds needed doing, Connie had learned when you need the dirt dished, you loaded Brid with Jack and coke, let her loose.

Now Connie looked at this Benjamin J., then looked at Brid and knew intuitively that Brid had been running her mouth.

Benjamin said,

"Brid and I had a convivial few drinks."

Then he giggled, mock admitted,

"So okay, we might have let the demons out more than we planned to."

Connie froze: This was very bad.

Benjamin moved fast, had his arm around Brid (very risky as Brid usually took the arm off anybody who touched her), said,

"But hey, no sin, no foul, we're on the same page, from Brid's little revelations. I surmise we might be kindred spirits."

Connie, used to regrouping fast, snarled,

"She's a dipso: Any mad shit she told you is the product of booze insanity."

Benjamin seemed delighted, echoed,

"*Dipso*, how wonderfully retro and yet not entirely off the mark"

Connie didn't like this guy. Everything about him creeped her out. If you've been chaplain at a women's prison and could still function, if erratically, it took major creep show to faze you.

She said,

"Thanks for dropping by but we're kind of busy right now."

Benjamin was still beaming, said,

"Bravo, good try, but, lady, you are so busted."

Connie looked at Brid, who seemed frozen in place, figured she'd have to handle this her own self, said,

"Let me be clear, like crystal clear. Fuck off."

Benjamin seemed to give this some thought, then said,

"No."

Connie was not used to the *no* word but it seemed every asswipe in Galway felt free to tell her that. Before she could unleash, Benjamin reached in the pocket of his very fine tweed coat, took out a fat packet, laid it gently before her, said,

"I would like to say this is a small donation but I'd be selling us short. It is indeed a sizable amount, the type that makes even a holy lady like your good self go *Holy shit*."

Connie, no qualms about cash, ripped it open, did a rapid count, looked up, did a recount, then said,

"Holy shit."

Benjamin smiled, mimicked a very poor Irish accent, said,

"'Tis but the beginning, me lady."

Connie felt a glow, the glow of opportunity, asked,

"The beginning of what?"

Like she could give a fuck, she was in, whatever mad plan he had.

Benjamin took out a calfskin wallet, pulled out a rush of notes, turned to Brid, asked,

"Be a sweetie, purchase us some happy libations, there's a good girl, while I natter with your boss."

Brid bristled.

Didn't take the notes, snarled,

"What am I, the message wanker?"

Benjamin reached over fast, pinched her cheek as you would a fat baby's, said,

"Thine own words hath described it so."

Connie said,

"Go do it."

In a tone that Brid had never refused. She tried,

"What's a fucking 'libation'?"

When she'd gone, Benjamin gave Connie what might actually be interpreted as a flirtatious grin and Connie, if cash dollars were on the horizon, would fuck a pope.

He produced a small book, said,

"If I may be so bold, I presumed to risk buying you a book."

Connie was intrigued and already feeling something of a hot flush, and phew-oh, that was a long time dormant. She said, coquettishly,

"As long as it's not Jane Austen, you're in with a shout."

Bang.

They were on each other.

Benjamin, as might be said, *gave good wood*.

Connie virtually swooned, screamed,

"You glorious animal."

From such random couplings have dynasties begun. See any story line in *Game of Thrones* as proof.

Think Lady Macbeth meets the psychopath from *The North Water*.

Spent, Connie fell back on the only comfortable armchair, gasped,

"What's the book?"

Benjamin, looking like he'd not a hair out of place, adjusted his trousers, crease intact, handed her

Scary Nuns.

Complete with photographs of "Brides of Christ" toting AK-47s.

Connie muttered,

"I think I'm in love."

"In
Greek
Tragedy
They
Fall
From
a
Great
Height.
In
Noir
They
Fall
From
the
Curb."

(Dennis Lehane)

Quotes of the week
February 24, 2019:

> "I heard on the radio that there was a win in Ireland and I caught the last three numbers. I checked the numbers online.
> And
> I was
> Numb."
> —375 million euro winner of the lottery

> "Sweatpants are a sign of defeat."
> —Karl Lagerfeld, RIP, aged eighty-five

> "By 'too big'
> I don't mean 'too famous.'
> I mean
> Too fat."
> —Edie Campbell on being dropped from Milan Fashion Week

> "I get up
> And then, you know,
> I sit down.
> I don't do none of this trotting around.
> I think it's bad for me."
> —Keith Richards on exercise

Benjamin and Connie were in bed again, after trysts

In/on.

The hallway.

The front garden.

The kitchen table (shades of *The Postman Always Rings Twice*).

And Brid sulked, drank, fumed, despaired, and raged.

Smashed furniture, slammed her head into the wall (headbanger?).

Wept.

Oh, wept bitter tears of abandonment.

Connie was oblivious and Benjamin could, if you'll forgive the pun, give a fuck.

Smoking in a rare moment away from their frenzy, Connie asked,

"Are you rich?"

He told the truth.

"Very."

She was thrilled, asked,

"How?"

For the second time in years, he told the truth, said,

"I'm a forensic accountant, a financial investigator: I do some very creative shady bookkeeping for extremely shady folk."

She mulled that over, then,

"Isn't it dangerous?"

He laughed, said,

"God, I hope so."

She now flat-out fucking adored him. He asked,

"You like movies?"

Oh, yeah.

He said,

"I liked *They Shoot Horses, Don't They?*

She didn't know it, said,

"Loved it."

He knew she lied, but so what?

He said,

"I'm working on a new version, *They burn horses, don't they?*

She sat up, went,

"Whoa, what?"

He said,

"We have two guys in common who busted our balls."

When she said nothing, he said,

"The deadbeat drunk Taylor and his sidekick, a psycho biker named Keefer."

She was very attentive now, said simply,

"And?"

He got out of bed, stretched, said,

"Those assholes hang out on some version of a ranch or farm outside town."

He turned, stroked her cheek, said,

"At the risk of mutating an American saying, I intend for them to 'buy the farm.'"

She stroked the long nasty scar all down his right leg, said,

"Count me in, lover."

He began to dress, carefully, as if it were important.

Perhaps it was.

He reached in his jacket, took out a long match, handed it to her.

She said,

"Lemme guess: We're a match."

An almost satanic look flitted briefly across his face, then was gone.

But

She'd seen it.

As the saying goes,

"Once seen!"

She was Californian, knew her satanic shit, knew it close.

He asked,

"Know what that is?"

Fuck, she thought, this is thin ice, tried,

"A long match."

He snarled,

"Don't be frivolous."

She was just a wee bit afraid but she knew she could break his neck fast; being a prison chaplain has its perks. Letting a trace of edge leak over her own tone, she said,

"It's a fucking long wooden match, with a red tip."

She nearly added,

And how drearily phallic.

But bit down.

The guy had cash so she could play it a little, said,

"It's your calling card."

Bingo.

He planted a wet kiss on her cheek.

Downstairs, Brid, listening, wearing a T with the hashtag, "MeatToo."

Spat.

Twice.

"What I would call a supernatural and mystical experience
    Has
    In its essence
    Some note
    Of a direct spiritual contact.
    Liberties
    A kind of flash or spark which ignites an intuition."

    (from a letter by Thomas Merton to Aldous Huxley)

Cynics pointed out that Merton died as the result of an electric fire that flashed or sparked.
    A disillusioned ex-priest postulated,
    "*Did Merton have a final epiphany before he burned*
    Or indeed
    As he burned?"

I was in Ollie Crowe's bar in Bohermore. The talk was of the murder of Clodagh, a lovely woman in the Midlands. She seemed to have the Irish dream: three gorgeous boys, a devoted husband who was not only a school vice principal but a major figure in the GAA, active in the community.

But.

Beware that fucking *but*.

He seemed to never leave Clodagh's side, even went with her and her sister to select Clodagh's wedding dress.

Creepy, right?

He would never allow Clodagh to have even a cup of tea with her beloved mother without him present. He was, as they say, *stuck in everything*.

Clodagh, deeply troubled, told her mother that he was in trouble at the school for missing money and something of a sexual nature. He had been wearing Clodagh's underwear and admitted he watched porn obsessively but Clodagh asserted he was *getting counseling*.

Yeah, right.

The night before he was due to return to work to, as they say, *face the music*, he crept up behind Clodagh, who was at the computer, planning a family holiday. He took her head nearly clean off with the ax, then he went upstairs, cut the vocal cords of the eldest boy lest he alert the two younger lads who shared a room; a knife was used, and the coroner stated there were signs of defensive wounds.

Fuck.

He then went into the other children's room and slit their throats; they were six and four. Back downstairs to transfer his wife's money into his account, then calmly wrote a five-page letter (that, even three years later, Clodagh's family have not been allowed to see in its entirety).

Gets worse, if possible.

His brother was to have his car, and he demanded that he *not be forgiven.*

As Brenda Power wrote in the *Sunday Times* to that last bit, "*Don't fucking worry!*"

She also added, to the pride of the pub, *May he rot in hell.*

A-fucking-men to that.

She ridiculed the notion that he'd *snapped.*

It was obvious he'd been planning for months as, months before, he moved the furniture so that Clodagh would be sitting with her back to him when he attacked her. He was a big man and she a petite woman.

The piss-poor coward.

But what irked her and only one other brave journalist was the *Rehabilitation of the predator syndrome.*

This was all the rage, if you'll excuse the horrendous pun. In this case, the priest praised the killer as a community person, a committed family man (seriously, like fuck that), a pillar of the community.

Clodagh's mother and sister broke their silence to appear on *Prime Time*, beg the powers that be (and don't) pleading for the *why* of it; his five-page letter still hadn't been released to them.

Clodagh's mother revealed in heart-wrenching detail the morning she went to Clodagh's house, with a feeling of dread, a note on the door, warned,

"Call the police."

I had to literally shut my ears, it was so agonizing to hear. There was a man sitting next to me. He looked cold, freezing. He asked me,

"Where would I get a hot water bottle?"

I said,

"1957."

March 4, 2019:

Keith Flint took his own life; the video of his band Prodigy's "Firestarter" is a sight to behold.

Luke Perry died, from a stroke at fifty-two; his career had recently rebooted with *Riverdale*.

The inventor of spell check died yesterday. May he roost in piece.

The Children

Children of the Galway miracle.
 Bannered the red top papers.
 In bold emphatic headlines, they screeched,
 Where are they?
   Who are they?
     Where did they come from?
 The journalists had no answers to the above
 But
 They speculated wildly; it's their raison d'être.
 Later, oh, so much later, they would be known as
 "The children of the lie."

Sara and Salazar were not siblings, but they were related through
 Brutality
 Pain
 Abuse
 Torture
 Terror.
 Sara was part of the above in a sly, subtle fashion.
 Sara was sixteen or eighteen but, in the ways of the world,
she was middle-aged.

She had developed a chameleon ability to alter her appearance so that she always seemed younger then she was. The drug Eltroxin kept her body as a perpetual girl. No physical development. She found it worked to lower the defenses of the predators and she viewed the world as dominated by the predatory.

She was intent on being the most ferocious of that breed.

Salazar was small and traumatized.

To Sara, he was disposable, as were all the others.

They had been thrown together when a line of refugees were swept up by U.S. border guards then, in a series of errors, they were put on a boat to Europe, landing in Greece, on the island of Kos, where Concern, the Irish charity, rescued a group of children.

More travel. The children had bonded by then and it was just taken as fact that they were siblings. Sal didn't speak, ever, such was the degree of his trauma. Sara protected him with a ferocity that was almost lethal. She knew how to handle a blade and was rarely without one. Her appearance of utter innocence lured many to mistake her as not only younger but harmless.

She'd been reared in Guatemala and her proudest memory was the trick she'd learned with blue light and a tattoo that spiraled up her left arm. It was of a cobra about to strike and when she bent her arm it gave the illusion of the snake in motion.

She had in her journey three previous "siblings." She'd slit each one's throat when they annoyed her.

Sara adapted fast to new surroundings and in the Galway refugee center the inmates were shown a series of religious movies by a bored and misguided nun.

In rapid succession Sara saw such gems as:

The Miracle of Lourdes.

The Secrets of Fatima.

Medjugorje Wonders.

Saw an opportunity.

Then found a leaflet about a dying Irish village, Ballyfin, desperate for a miracle. She knew she'd found her final nirvana.

Persuaded Sal to actually speak, just one sentence, and short,

"La Madonna"

Sara had once actually had a sort of mother, at least a woman who lived long enough to name her. In the days before she died (during an attack among the refugees by a *cleansing* squad), she had told her of Camargue.

The Camargue in southern France, an hour's drive from Marseille, or if you are fleeing then maybe a lifetime.

A group of people constantly on the move or run has its antecedent in
Les Saintes-Maries-de-la-Mer.
A region of
Gypsies.
Lagoons.
Black bulls.
Flamingos.

White horses.
It possessed a ferocious kind of beauty that was almost threatening
in its fierceness.
So many displaced persons fled there that it was known as the Gypsy
Pilgrimage.

According to legend, the Three Marys, witnesses to the Resurrection, were set adrift in a boat from Palestine in AD 45.

With them was their servant Sara.

Sara remained in Camargue, built the church, was buried there.

Every year, bands of Gypsies crowd into the church to pay homage to Sara.

The woman, before she was murdered, said to Sara,

"You will be the one the Gypsies,

The outcasts.

The discarded will worship you but you must give them a miracle."

In Guatemala, Sara found the blue magic trick of light, knew she just had to wait to find her very own Camargue.

Along the way, she found her own murderous nature; she would be the legendary Sara, with a killer twist.

I'd been watching *Durham County*.

Fuck, it was dark, darker even than *Ozark*.

Weird things had happened to me since/because of my accident.

My limp had virtually disappeared, my bad hearing had improved significantly, and the phantom pains in the mutilated right hand were definitely gone.

Miracles?

Fuck knows but I knew enough to ride any gift horse for all it's worth.

And okay, I'll fess up: I did a Matt Scudder, meaning I gave tithe to the Church.

And golly, gosh, as fools say, I recited the Our Father daily.

I even added the Protestant rider to it,

> "*For thine is the kingdom,*
> *And the power,*
> *And the glory.*"

If God turned out to be Protestant, I'd be covered and, God knows, bigger turnarounds have occurred. Look at Brexit.

But how was the three-pronged investigation proceeding?

Keefer had met and threatened Benjamin J., our suspected arsonist; he also met and threatened the wife beater/killer.

My part, find the children. Nope.

Not yet.

Monsignor Rael, the Vatican hatchet man, was almost daily harassing me, stressing the amount of money he'd given me.

Maybe I should have gotten Keefer to threaten him.

I continued to exercise ferociously to regain some muscle and energy, and, hold the goddamn phones, I was even taking "African mango."

It supposedly had terrific restorative powers.

Mainly, it was cheap, like my own self.

Twenty-third of March, we got a few days of nigh summer weather.

As I said, weird all round.

Salthill

In Irish Bóthar na Trá is a seaside area in Galway.

Lying within the townland of Lenaboy.

In the 1930s

Salthill was known as

"The village."

The Salthill church was built as an outside church in 1938.

In many ways, the whole area of Salthill is *other*.

If you were born in the actual city, chances are you would never set foot in that church.

I never did until after I met a man named Morgan.

I have not been there since.

One of the great joys of Galway is to stand on the sand at Salthill, gaze out at Galway Bay, imagine the U.S. just over the frontier, to have that almost pleasurable yearning, for what I've never known, and maybe that's part of the appeal.

Early March, who you gonna see?

Dog walkers. Dogs are not banned from the beach until June. People should be banned the rest of the time. Galway City Council were busy fighting over the fact that there were no more graves available in Bohermore (unless you came from money and influence, preferably both).

Bids were already in from firms to have a state-of-the-art crematorium.

Burn, baby, burn.

Dare I say, my dad would have turned in his grave?

I'd burn for sure, before and after.

I'd like to be thrown in the bay.

Especially as I'd thrown various thugs in there over the years. I kid thee not at all.

At the kiosk end of the beach were the stricken remnants of a hen party, a sad to saddest sigh. You could almost smell the Jägermeister, the de rigueur bombshell drink. I needn't worry about them for a bit as no stir from the scattered bodies.

A man was watching me from the promenade, as if contemplating me or the ocean or both; he definitely seemed to be on the verge of some quandary.

Finally, he hopped from the prom onto the beach, walked determinedly toward me. I hoped I wouldn't have to kick the shit out of him. It was not only too early but too peaceful.

So far.

Reaching me, he asked,

"Jack Taylor?"

Never, ever a good start. I always wanted to go movie-wise, snap,

"Who wants to know?"

He put out his hand, said,

"I'm Stephen Morgan, and I need your help."

I sighed, thinking,

Aw, just fuck off.

But went with

"Sorry, I'm all out of helping folk."

Didn't faze him. He reached in his jacket, a fine Hugo Boss leather field jacket, took out a stack of notes, large denomination, said,

"Take this, just a few days of your time."

I took the money. Maybe I could buy a jacket like his. I asked,

"What's the problem?"

He took out a packet of Marlboro, offered me one, I took it, and he fired us up with a well-bruised Zippo, said,

"I was off them for twenty years."

Like I gave a fuck, but I said,

"Like the rest of us poor fucks."

He was in his late forties, jet-black hair in need of a cut, a face that had endured sorrow and recently. He had a look of Tom Hardy but way thinner. His voice was more from learning than genes. He said,

"My daughter, Meredith, has suffered horrendously from trolls, one in particular who goes by the hashtag *diebitchsoon*.

At first I thought he was speaking German until I broke it down.

Die.

Bitch.

Soon.

Jesus wept.

I asked,

"What age is Meredith?"

He looked like he was having either a stroke or a heart attack, or both.

I put out my hand, held his shoulder, took my emergency small travel flask out of my 501s, said,

"Drink this."

He looked amazed, asked,

"You carry booze?"

I tried a smile, said,

"And a good thing I do. Drink."

He did.

Then coughed and shuddered, gasped,

"The fuck is that?"

"Salvation."

He near whispered,

"Meredith was eleven."

Past dreaded tense.

Few minutes later, he stood almost straight, said,

"I have tried everything to find out who the demon is, but no luck."

I asked,

"The Guards?"

He scoffed, near spat, said,

"Cyberbullying they told me is rampant."

Indeed.

The papers carried horror stories of such daily.

He said,

"Meredith gave me a navy wool tie for my birthday. It was kind of a joke as she knows I hate ties and she had it inscribed with *it's not my thing*."

Fuck.

I said lamely,

"Sounds like a great girl."

"Was, she was a great girl, the best."

Oh, God, but I had to ask finally as the past tense again came up.

"How do you mean?"

A small tear rolled down his cheek, the cheeks flushed from the booze. It landed softly on the sand, like an abandoned prayer. He said,

"She's dead. And I swore to her that I would not only find the bastard but ensure he never bothered her again."

Then he near shrieked,

"I didn't find him. He actually increased his campaign of terror as if he knew I was trying to find him or maybe her, who the fuck knows these days."

I had nothing so said nothing.

With supreme effort he said,

"On her own birthday, she hung herself in her bedroom."

Pause.

"With the navy tie."

He rolled up his sleeve, said,

"I was so insane with grief that I got a tattoo. You think I got my daughter's name?"

I thought so.

He said,

"You'd be wrong."

Showed me his arm.

In bold Gothic script was

D.

B.

S.

A *miracle*

Is defined as a
Wonder,
A marvel,
A marvelous event due to supernatural agency.

One of the mysteries of Galway is a curious thing on the clock over Galway Camera and what it says.

It says *Dublin Time*.

The fact that now the clock shows ordinary winter time only adds to the mystery.

Not so long ago Galwegians, delighting in the longer days of sunlight than in Dublin and displaying an oddity that makes living in Galway a pleasure, set their clocks a full eleven and a half minutes behind Dublin.

Of course, this plays into the Dublin belief that Galway is/ was behind and not just in minutes.

I was standing under said clock when Jimmy Higgins came along; a radio broadcaster, terrific musician, and possessed of a sharp wit.

He handed me a double CD and said,

"It's old style."

Just what I love. I said,

"Jimmy, nowadays they say *old school*."

He looked baffled, asked,

"Why?"

Indeed.

I attempted,

"They want to change the name of everything now and, get this, get rid of the Angelus."

Jimmy had written a beautiful book about the show-band era, titled,

"*Are Ye the Band?*"

He asked how I was after my accident.

I said,

"They called it a miracle."

He pondered that, giving me that Tuam look of utter frankness, then,

"You appear in fine fettle. I suppose all the hurling you did stood to you."

Jimmy was that rare to rarest individual—he saw the good in you, little as it was. He added.

"Well, mind yourself Jack, there are few of us left."

And getting fewer by the day.

I took a measured stroll down the town, passed the bronze seated statues of two writers, on a bench, a distance of two feet between them; one was Edward Carson and the other, well, he was what the locals call *a total*.

Shorthand for "total stranger."

I looked in the window of the Treasure Chest; all the goods displayed cost a small fortune to even contemplate.

As a child of poverty, I remember when it was Glynn's, what my mother called a "dear" place, meaning it wasn't dear in the sense of sentimental but fierce expensive.

It was fierce.

For weeks there was a beautiful replica of the *Titanic*, in each and every correct detail, down to the doomed lifeboats: It filled me with wonder.

It cost ninety-five pounds, in what is now known as "old" money before the curse of the euro. The china factory that employed a quarter of the town had a weekly wage of two pounds, ten shillings, and that was with overtime.

A union?

Yeah, dream on.

My father, who worked like an African American on the railway, earned one pound, twenty shillings.

But, oh my God, money felt like money. A half crown was not only a fine sum but the coin, it felt like wealth; eight of them and you had a mighty pound.

A woman I knew vaguely stopped, asked,

"What are thinking of, Jack?"

I gave her what passed for a not unfriendly smile, said,

"I was wondering what I'd buy with ninety pounds?"

She discreetly backed away, her look screaming.

"'Tis early to be drunk."

* * *

My former lady friend/significant other, whatever the hell the *fluid* term is now, had previously introduced me to

"Danny Doherty."

From Derry—no, not London Derry—and for odd reasons we became friends, despite Marion, my ex, telling him I was toxic.

Thing is, I agreed with her on that.

Most of my friends were in the graveyard and, yes, because of me, directly or not.

I may not have put them there but I sure paved the road.

Danny was a whiz in an IT company, made serious cash but seemed like he *hadn't a shilling.* The best kind of wealth, the nonshowy type.

I saw him making his way past a busker who was mauling "The Fields of Athenry." Danny gave him some money, smiled when he saw me, said,

"Jeez, he must really hate that song."

He was five-foot-ten, weighed 160 pounds, was gym fit and looked like a benevolent bouncer. Sounds crazy but then this is Galway. His only concession to being rich was his clothes, discreet but oh so freaking classy.

A cap that made him seem handsome.

He wasn't.

Chinos with a permanent crease, no mean achievement, one of those tweed coats called Tru Dry, truly expensive. (I checked one time in Anthony Ryan's; they were as dear as the ship in Glynn's from my youth.)

And shoes, ah, the shoes.

Keen boots.

Small fortune, they say.

My Doc Martens went blacker with envy. We shook hands and he asked,

"Fancy a pint?"

I did and mostly do.

We were at a table in the Imperial Hotel, at the top of Eyre Square, once a late night pit stop for the Guards, as it was quiet.

We had boilermakers as 'tis not often we get to chat.

I managed to pay first, an Irish gig where friends near fight to buy the first round. You have to be quick or not, depending on whether you're a mean fuck.

Danny said,

"I was sick to my stomach about Christchurch."

The day before, a gunman, Australian, twenty-eight years old, entered two mosques, murdered forty-eight people, one a boy of five. He wore a live cam on his head, feeding his sick supporters live commentary as he killed and mowed down the innocent. He then got in his car, blasted out the side window with a shotgun, continued to shoot at passersby. He had, as these psychos do, written a long manifesto, which, along with the video footage, was available for twenty-four hours after the carnage.

There are no words.

I had no words.

Danny sighed, said,

"I don't know this world anymore."

Me neither.

To ease the darkness, I said,

"They arrested McGregor again in Florida for criminal battery."

Danny said,

"Next time he gets in the cage for a fight, may they lock it with intent."

Amen.

I said,

"Danny, I need some help."

He nodded, said,

"Tell me."

I did, outlined the death of Meredith Morgan, her father's grief, even the tattoo on his arm, how the Guards were already swamped with cyber theft, bullying, the whole new dizzying array of crimes the Internet was spewing out.

He listened attentively, even took out a slim black leather notebook, a Cross pen, jotted down the details. Then he looked up, said,

"The dark web is a scary place and difficult to track. You break through one firewall, six more are behind it, and they have nigh perfected the art of redirecting, or rather misdirecting."

Not reassuring but I asked,

"Can it be done?"

He smiled, almost weary, said,

"Oh, yeah, if they are there, they can be found, but it takes time."

I dreaded asking, but

"How much time?"

He considered, then,

"A month, if we get lucky and especially if the sick fuck gets arrogant."

I caught the barman's eye, did the finger thing they understand, said to Danny,

"It's expensive."

He waited until the round came, then,

"For friends, money is not a factor."

I asked,

"Will you do it?"

He nodded, said,

"One thing you need to understand. I said it could take at least a month but I was talking in general terms."

I waited.

"But me, say twenty-four hours."

The whole day had just shaped up, I asked,

"You want to get some dinner? They do fine bacon and cabbage here, like in the old days."

He said,

"And ruin a fine building buzz with food, no way."

I agreed.

Later, as we unsteadily wound our merry way toward taxicabs, Danny put his arm on my shoulder, asked,

"I don't want to put a damper on a fine evening but . . ."

He was going to put the damper on.

He asked,

"When I find this troll, and I will find them, what then?"

I had thought about that, thought about it a lot, then said, nearly truthfully,

"I was thinking a tattoo."

He gave me a look that showed the steel behind his good nature, said,

"I'm not sure what that entails but I don't think I want to speculate."

I shook his hand, firmly, not bone crushing but close, said,

"That's for the best."

"If
    You're
      Lucky
        Enough
          to
            Be
              Irish
                Then
                  You're
                    Lucky
                      Enough"

St. Patrick's Day.

A grand excuse for the world to drink like the Irish.

And, at least in Ireland, they kept the mad notion well oiled, excuse the drunken pun.

But.

But is always bad and here it is very dark and woesome.

In Tyrone, in Northern Ireland, a small hotel in a small village held its annual disco for mainly teens. A hundred turned up but then buses began arriving, spilling out nearly four hundred unexpected teenagers.

A ferocious crush/ push/ stampede ensued, and the hotel staff locked the doors. Teenagers, forced against the glass, begged to be allowed in; the staff refused.

Three kids were crushed to death.

Aged

Sixteen, seventeen, eighteen.

Horror engulfed the country.

In the days following, the hotel manager and one of the staff were arrested, charged with manslaughter. In a bizarre twist, the manager was arrested on drug charges when a white powder was found. Then, when tests revealed it to be not drugs, he was

De-arrested.

A term new to the population.

The three funerals took place on the Friday, in three separate churches, but the sight of a pink coffin for the lone girl did me in entirely.

The prime minister of New Zealand earned the respect of the world when she pledged in an address to the captured terrorist,

"We reject you; your name will never be uttered as long as I live."

No notoriety/infamy for the psycho.

On Saturday, Keefer and I met for a drink. He handed me a book.

Life

By Keith Richards.

Said,

"You want to know about the Stones, read this."

I actually didn't want to know a whole lot about them but said,

"Can't wait to read it."

He shrugged, asked,

"Dude, when are you coming back to the farm?"

I told him of the cyber bully and the sheer grief of the father.

Keefer thought on that, then,

"So, we have two miracle children to find, an arsonist we need to literally put out, and an asshole husband who killed his wife. Now you have this new case?"

We were drinking tequila, for no good reason, which might be the best excuse.

On the other side of my third, I was feeling crusade-ish, said,

"Once I find this cyber fuck, we'll deal with the other three cases."

Keefer had deep frown lines on his face, said,

"I have a real sense of impending doom."

I shrugged it off, said,

"Blame it on the tequila."

Maybe a little more flippant then I meant but it did sound like a blow off.

He stood up, said,

"No, Jack, it's not the booze, it's you."

Then, in a gesture that haunts me, he threw a rake of money on the table, said,

"Buy the next few on me."

And was gone.

Guns and Rosaries

I watched a documentary with the above title.

Narrated by Martin Sheen.

An incredible story.

Patrick Peyton, from a large, poor family in Mayo, wanted to be a priest.

The Irish crowd said,

"You are not educated enough."

So he went to the U.S.

Became a priest and then near died of tuberculosis, which was killing thousands of people in America. Near death, Patrick pledged if he recovered, he would devote his life to the Madonna and spreading the rosary.

He turned out to be a public relations genius.

He got the slogan,

"The family that prays together,

Stays together."

And hounded celebrities like Bing Crosby, Grace Kelly, Frank Sinatra, Maureen O'Hara to join his crusade of the family rosary. He said,

"Aim to get ten million families to say the rosary."

He did, trebled it, and was a rock star in his appearances.

His big task was South America, so enter the CIA, who funded his campaign.

Gave him a million dollars.

But.

The Church in the sixties, fearful of this money coming out, began to curb his appeal.

You might say,

"The Church that conspired together.

Prayed together."

Then I saw the documentary *The Family*, a massive network of politicians and businessmen whose tentacles reached all over the world. Their influence and power was staggering. Utilizing the National Prayer Breakfast, they had every U.S. president since Eisenhower in attendance and all this web spun by the most influential man you never heard of.

Douglas Coe.

His genius was to stay *invisible*, manipulating the name of Jesus, to cover a whole host of activities that remain mired in darkness and the shadows.

I had been to the cinema for the first time in years—Galway's new movie theater.

Theater was $8 million in debt, not that we needed a new one. We already had two Omniplex and the city was outraged at this white elephant.

The cinema itself was a maze of steep granite chairs and screens all over a confused site. *Chaotic* didn't even come near to the whole shambles.

But I wanted to see *Us*, the new one from the director of the brilliant *Get Out*.

Phew-oh.

Terrifying, topical, and oh, so relevant.

Put the heart sideways in me many times.

Lupita Nyong'o in a dual role was a sight to wonder at.

I came out shaken, nearly walked into a woman, friend of my late mother. My mother, the very hound from hell.

So any of her friends were never going to be chuffed (as they say in Hampstead) to meet me.

But she excelled herself, near spat,

"Is there anything sadder than a grown man having to go to the pictures on his own? Sure, who'd go anywhere with the likes of you?"

Normally, if "normal" has any meaning in the realm of the truly evil, I'd just pass on by.

But!

I got right in her face, snarled,

"My mother was a bad bitch but you? You might be just a little bit worse."

She took a step back, frightened, but the nastiness won out, she railed,

"I wish that truck had killed you."

Now that is true horror.

Who needs the cinema?

After an encounter like that, you need some balance. I went to Charlie Byrne's bookshop. It had just won

"Best Independent Bookshop in Ireland!"

I congratulated them; it was a pleasure to see them win. I bought

Emily Dean's

Everybody Died, So I Got a Dog.

Purely on the title. Noirin asked,

"You had a dog?"

Indeed.

Two.

Both died.

I didn't of course say that, in the midst of them delighted with their win.

Even I have some decency.

Danny Doherty called me, said he had news.

I felt part exhilaration, part dread.

If he had the name of the troll, what then?

Tell Stephen Morgan I knew who had terrorized his daughter into her grave?

I didn't know.

Danny was dressed to impress as usual: fine suit, expensive raincoat, he looked composed. We were in the Meyrick hotel; seemed apt for serious business. We ordered coffee, didn't speak until we'd settled. He had a file before him, said,

"Phew, this was a tough one, behind every firewall was another blind, then bounced back to three different locations."

I wasn't entirely sure what that entailed save it sounded difficult.

He opened the file, asked,

"You sure you want to know?"

I was.

I think.

He said,

"Okay, you'd expect a monster, at least in description, but it's a woman, girl really, twenty years old, lives with her parents, and gets social security. In appearance she seems almost normal, drab really, doesn't go down to the pub or hang with anyone."

I said,

"Spends her time frightening young vulnerable girls."

He considered that, then,

"Here's her photo and address."

She lived off Grattan Road, nice unremarkable house, a study in normalcy. The photo showed a girl rather than a woman, looking away from the camera, brown hair in long braids, a face that missed being pretty by a distance but makeup would have helped: Mostly, she looked young.

Her name was Greta Haut.

Unusual surname. The only time I'd ever come across it was the writer Woody Haut. Her parents were some sort of born-again Christians and belonged to a group that met on Wednesday nights where, it was said, some spoke in tongues. One wondered if any of them were civil.

Greta had been recruited by a top tech company but was let go for *unspecified reasons*. Like being a psycho, perhaps. She dressed like an ex-nun,

That is, unremarkable, mainly old green combat jacket, high-top sneakers.

She had never been in trouble with the law save for a minor charge of stealing a six-pack of Red Bull. Most of her time seemed to be spent at home, destroying lives.

I said,

"A winner."

Danny gave me a look of mild distaste, said,

"The wee lass is obviously unhinged."

Lass!

That infuriated me. I snarled,

"Lass! She's a full-formed psychotic bitch who gets off on tormenting vulnerable girls."

Danny physically pulled back, as if I'd slapped him, said,

"Whoa, get a grip."

I bit down for a moment, trying to rein it in, tried,

"I'm just a little tired of excusing sick fucks that ruin others."

Danny was done, stood up, said,

"I better go. I hope you won't do something criminal here."

I offered,

"Let me pay you for your time."

"No."

I had preparations to make for Greta Haut. In a dive bar off the docks, I bought some Rohypnol, the date rape drug. The guy who sold it to me didn't bat an eyelid, then went to get a single bottle of Coke, screw-off top.

I also got a large knife, known as the Bowie blade, which had a serrated edge that would put shivers on a corpse.

Wednesday evening Greta's parents would be attending their prayer meeting. I put my purchases in a small backpack, dressed in black jeans, black T, and threw in an old tie that had attended more funerals than I dare remember.

I broke into Greta's house at eight that evening. No sophisticated locks; I guess born-agains are more trusting. The house was plainly furnished, attesting to tidiness more than money. I crept up the stairs, could hear the white noise of Greta's PC. Her door was ajar. I pushed it open carefully.

Her back was to me, headphones on: She was dressed in sweatpants, sloppy sweatshirt. I tapped her gently on the shoulder. She nigh jumped a foot, screamed once. I gripped her hair, said,

"Scream again and I'll kill you."

I pulled up my backpack, produced the bottle of Coke, my own flask, offered her the Coke, asked, as I offered the flask,

"You want something stronger in the Coke?"

She shook her head, her eyes wide but a nasty malevolence creeping in. I said,

"*Sláinte.*"

She asked,

"Is there poison in it?"

I gave her my best smile, all wolves, said,

"The only poison here is you."

She took a large gulp from the Coke, so step one done. She seemed to ease with the sugar rush, asked,

"Are you going to rape me?"

I said,

"Good Lord, no."

I leaned back as if relaxing, then sprang forward, gave her one almighty lash to the face. Few things on earth pack such devastating heft. As she reeled back, I took out the rope, tied her securely to the chair, took out the tie.

Shoved it in her face, said,

"This is the tie Meredith hanged herself with. You can keep it."

As she began to droop, I said,

"I am going to carve the initials you like so much into your forehead, slowly and large."

She managed,

"No, my face is my best feature."

I looked at her, said,

"You're even more deluded than I thought."

Then, she was out.

I had to force blank my feelings, because so much of me wanted to kill her.

I swept her laptop off the desk, allowing my full rage to knock it clear across the room. The desk was a beautiful oak; gorgeous, really.

I took the knife and carved deliberately and with malice flowing,

D.

B.

S.

When her parents returned, them being Christian, they could express shock in the many tongues they'd acquired and no doubt attribute the deed to the devil.

They wouldn't be entirely wrong.

"If the monks and nuns
Are not living a life of constant prayer,
Or at least striving to,
Then their lives are a waste
And a scandal.

Let this monastery be sold
And the money
Be given to the poor."

(Fr. Basil Pennington, abbot and writer, 1966)

Connie had a week of near bliss due to Benjamin J.

He wined, dined, and bedded her with élan.

She'd never had such attention before. The only flaw in the gorgeous setup was Brid. Brid who seemed to hate Benjamin with ferocity and glared at him with burning eyes, eyes of naked resentment. He seemed to thrive on her bile, would pat her head and whisper,

"Good dog, you're such a loyal dope."

Connie tried to subtly rein him in, suggested,

"Darling, maybe ease up on the teasing."

He gave that radiant smile that lit her heart, said,

"Ah, it's because I love her."

Uh-huh.

Brid fantasized about putting a knife in his black heart, twisting it as she got right in his face, screamed,

"Who's a dog? Who's a fucking dog now?"

He scolded her,

"Have you found the children? You can't just sit on yer ass, welch off my largesse. There's a limit to even my big heart."

Then he winked at her.

A Friday evening, he said to Connie,

"My love, I've booked a table for us at Milano's, so dress, like, *hot*."

She swooned, went all coy, then saw the disgust on Brid's face. She took a risk, asked,

"Um, what about Brid? Maybe we should take her along, just this once?"

He looked at Brid with what might actually have seemed like benevolence but was anything but. He said,

"Brid, my not-so-busy little bee, how about I give you some cash, treat yourself to a bottle of Baileys or some other sweet shit you crave?"

Before she could raise enough vigor to spit in his face, he peeled off some euros, seemed to consider, and then dropped a ten note on the floor, said,

"Maybe a few miniatures of Baileys. We need you sharp."

Brid stormed out, the ten note abandoned like a useless invocation.

That evening, in Milano's, Connie was dressed in a slinky black number and, to her satisfaction, turned some heads. Benjamin J. was dressed in a well-cut black suit, a white shirt that gleamed, his hair neatly trimmed. They presented a picture of fulfilled ambition.

Connie had the house special, a spaghetti Bolognese that was the best she'd ever tasted and—fuck calories—she had garlic bread to mop up the delicious sauce. She paused mid-bite with the bread, asked Benjamin, because of the garlic,

"Will we be kissing later?"

He gave his demure smile, not a mile from a grimace, said,

"You betcha but the garlic will add a kick."

He had the sirloin steak, baked potato, demolished the lot with short, sharp-focused bites, ordered a second bottle of wine, and, as they sat back, he raised his glass, said,

"To the flames we engulf."

A lot of the time, she'd little idea what the fuck he was talking about but it all sounded sexy so who cared? She said,

"Burn, indeed."

He produced a long match, red top, and the bottom half of the match appeared to be enclosed in silver, said,

"This is our special match, nonsafety of course. It is to commemorate the beginning of your fame and riches."

She took the match, examined it. He asked,

"What do you want? Shall I tell you?"

She nodded, half blitzed from the wine and the whole gig.

He ordered espressos with a hint of Grenadine to spice them. He said,

"To be famous, rich, revered, and, best of all, a hero. Sound good?"

Good?

Sounded bloody fantastic to Connie. She took a moment to gather herself, asked,

"What will it take?"

He rose from the table, said in sultry tone,

"Walk with me."

Nodded to the waitress, to indicate smoke break, got outside, produced a pack of Lucky Strikes, the irony of the title of the cigs a source of added fun to him. He took out two, looked at Connie, and said,

"Woman, what's the matter? Strike the match."

She got it on the first flick, fired them up. He said,

"You're a natural."

She beamed.

He took a few rapid drags, then ground the cig under his heel with vehemence, said,

"Here's the deal. To be great, sacrifice is required. Are you prepared to suffer to be magnificent?"

She nodded, already in so deep that she'd have given him a BJ there and then. He continued,

"Here's the plan. I know where the children are being kept. Brid in her cups told me you said the only feature all the shrines lacked was the death of the visionaries. Well, we're going to provide that, to set a fire of biblical beauty, and here's the tough part. You, in attempting to rescue the blessed children, will be burned in your heroics—nothing too serious but enough to muster deep sympathy. You will lose your dearest friend in the attempt, your devoted ally who gives her life to try and rescue those poor mites. You, in burnt clothes, will try for actual smoke still rising from your clothes. You will be on the front pages of all the papers. Your message from the children, their last dying plea, to build a shrine for them and your fallen comrade."

Connie was shocked. She'd seen or heard just about every callous act on the planet but this took her breath away.

Benjamin read her hesitation, said,

"Or not. Just crawl back into your tiny world of being nobody."

She heard the steel leak over his tone. She knew if she refused, the very fact of her knowing his plan put her in a lethal position. She tried,

"Brid has been at my side through the bad years. Does she have to, um, go?"

Benjamin sighed, looked to the sky, said,

"Only fire is reliable, the only sure element."

He walked into the restaurant, laid a stack of bills on the table, then came back out, didn't even look at Connie, strolled away.

She wasn't entirely sure but she thought he was whistling.

Connie felt utterly defeated, the feeling of floating, being enchanted as she'd been over the last weeks, evaporated. She got back to the tent. The so-called new convent she'd had such plans for . . . She sank into a chair, muttered,

"I need a flaming miracle."

You might say her plea was weirdly heard—if not from above, from someplace way darker, as Brid staggered into the tent very drunk and spoiling for a fight. She saw Connie, snarled,

"The whore of Babylon."

It was at that moment
That they would feel the presence of the devil
And beg God
To come, deliver them from him.
It was that moment
I made them see
That they finally realized
That God had been there all along.
It was then that they realized
That the devil
Is just God
In his night attire.

(Craig Russell, *The Devil Aspect*)

Keefer and I were sitting on the rocks overlooking Galway Bay. It was one of those fine crisp March mornings, you almost felt optimistic. We'd a flask of one of Keefer's sour mash whiskeys and, like old cowboys, were sipping it from tin cups.

Why?

Why, indeed?

Because Keefer had shown up at my apartment with the above items and suggested we sit *by the dock of the bay*. He was dressed in a seriously battered fringe suede jacket—something Fleetwood Mac might have used in their heyday—battered waistcoat, Willie Nelson bandanna, motorcycle boots. As usual, he looked like an extra from *Easy Rider*.

He had covered all the musical genres with old Hollywood movies riding point.

He said,

"I've been reading."

Showstopper.

What do you say but

"What?"

He pulled out a battered paperback from one of his numerous pockets, handed it over.

Honky Tonk Samurai, by Joe Lansdale

I knew enough to know it was about book twelve or so in the Hap and Leonard series, featuring a white trash guy and a large black gay man who solved crimes in glorious and violent fashion. I said,

"It's a TV series now."

He looked at me, said,

"You're shitting me."

"Nope, with James Purfoy and Michael Williams."

He savored that a minute and found nothing to like, asked,

"Purfoy—isn't that dude English?"

Before I could reply, he said,

"Anyhow, talk about serendipity or such shit, the preface to the book is like spooky. Here, take a look."

Having no idea what he meant I took the book, read this at the beginning of chapter 1:

> *Just when you think*
> *You got things learned good*
> *And life's flowing right,*
> > *A damn Mack truck comes along*
> > *And runs your highly attractive*
> > *Ass over.*

I said,

"It sure is odd."

Lame, right?

The rocks we were sitting on are about a swim from the main beach. The small stretch of sand below us is usually empty but a young man appeared, held up a stick, threw it, shouted,

"Fetch!"

Nothing unusual there save there was no sign of a dog. Then he walked to the stick, said, "Good dog," and picked up the stick, repeated the process.

Keefer said,

"See that there, one of the reasons I love this city. You can be stone cold insane, bonkers, as they say in the country formerly known as Britain, but as long as you keep the craziness to your own self no one bats an eye."

The guy spotted us, stared at us a moment, asked,

"Why are you drinking out of tin cups?"

I nearly said,

Same reason you're walking an imaginary dog.

But sense prevailed as it's never a great idea to fuck with someone's illusion; no good comes of it.

Keefer said,

"We're worried about the environment. Styrofoam ruins the ecological balance."

The guy was distracted by a sign near the main beach that warned,

"No dogs allowed on the beach during the summer months."

He looked at me, asked,

"What month is this?"

I said,

"You're good, summer is ages away."

He switched his eyes to Keefer, asked,

"You do realize your mate is not all in it."

Keefer, enjoying the whole episode of weirdness, said,

"But it's Galway, madness is okay."

The guy shook his head as if freeing it from us, then turned on his heel, parting with,

"If you find my dog, there's a reward."

Keefer and I were in the GBC, the only real restaurant in the city if you wanted a serious fry-up, the whole carbohydrate neon nightmare, the type of food that you believe soaks up the booze. Well, you don't really buy that but you have the false appetite that early-day drinking provides.

I knew Frank the chef from way back. He had two dogs and tended to them better than most anyone I know. We were sitting at the window table, the city up close and almost personal.

The waitress approached with caution. Keefer has that effect but then he smiles and charm ensues. He said to her,

"How are you?"

She blushed.

When do you ever see that anymore?

She managed to say,

"I'm well, thank you."

I said,

"Could I get

Eggs, fried soft.

Sausages.

Rashers.

Toast.

Pot of tea?"

Keefer let out a sigh, said,

"Dude, that's hard core."

Then to the waitress,

"I'll risk the same with an ambulance standing by."

She stood for a moment, then walked away, uncertainty in her stride.

Keefer asked,

"Tea, really?"

I tried to explain to him that with a fry-up tea is the only rider. He wasn't convinced but let it slide, asked,

"You ever coming back to the country?"

I said,

"I'd like to find those kids of the so-called miracle."

Keefer thought about that, said,

"That leaves three cases—the abusive murdering husband, the arsonist, and the troll who caused the death of the teenager."

"Two,"

I said.

The food came. It looked like a veritable avalanche of food. Keefer said,

"Fuck, wish we'd stayed on the rocks."

He made a halfhearted attempt to eat but the sheer amount seemed to defeat him. He asked the waitress for a pot of strong black coffee, then to me said,

"You took care of one of them. I kind of hope it wasn't the arsonist. I'd like to deal with him personally."

I said,

"The troll."

He drank some coffee, seemed restored, asked,

"How?"

I really didn't want to relive it due to a blend of guilt and horror over the lengths I had gone to, so I said simply,

"I marked her card."

Benjamin J. prided himself on his car, a black Bentley, over twenty years old, in pristine condition. He kept it in a garage off the Grattan Road. He rarely drove it as it did tend to draw attention. Alongside it was a very battered pickup truck, so beat-up it was hard to even gauge its color. This was, as he termed it,

"His business truck."

If he ever got nicked, the pickup contained all the evidence necessary to convict him. The risk of that added to its faded allure. Connie stood beside him now as he put various items in the truck. He watched her as she admired the Bentley.

He handed her a set of keys, said,

"Knock yourself out."

She looked at him, asked,

"Really?"

He gave her the wolf smile, said,

"What's mine is yours, dear."

She got behind the wheel, turned the ignition, and felt a stirring as the engine roared. Since meeting Benjamin J. she was in a haze of simmering heat.

She looked at the truck, asked,

"You planning on some building?"

He laughed, said,

"Exactly the opposite. This is more about destructing."

Yet again she'd no idea what he meant but loved the way he said it. He gave her a smile of utter malevolence, asked,

"So want to burn shit down?"

She thought,

God help me, I'm up for everything, even the sacrifice of Brid.

When I was a little girl
I used to dress my Barbie in a nun's habit
So she could beat the hell out of Skipper
And not get in trouble.

(Brynn Harris, comedian)

Tiger Woods won the Masters, staging one of the greatest comebacks of all time. On the twelfth hole of the final round, the leader board was a mess of contenders vying for the top spot. You could almost see Tiger look at it, steel himself, think,

Enough of this shit.

And an electric buzz ran through the crowd as Tiger seemed to change. The energy was almost tangible as he bit down and intimidated the wannabes, took the title to huge cheers. The trauma, pain, sordid stories all seemed to fade away as Tiger exploded with joy when he sank the winning putt.

So redemption was possible.

One of the commentators said,

"It's a miracle."

I was in Crowe's pub when Tiger sank that putt and even guys who hated him rose to cheer.

It took the focus off the lead national story: the president of the FAI, Delaney, tried to get a superinjunction to prevent details getting out of his *lending* the football association 100,000 euros.

This opened the door to details of lavish spending, the usual rackets most often associated with the charities. In a rapidly escalating farce, Delaney resigned as president, created the position of vice executive president, and—guess what?—appointed his own good self to this position.

The tragedy of all this thievery was the grassroots clubs, struggling to pay for the most basic amenities.

The Church, meanwhile, as shocking details emerged about the beloved Bishop Casey, revealed the affable popular bishop to be one of the most horrendous child abusers.

At first, even his most ardent supporters, though reeling in horror, refused to believe it, but the landslide of evidence proved the allegations. The last folk hero of the people was a monster all along.

A very bitter pill to swallow in Galway, which had defended him all those years.

A guy beside me in Crowe's, reading the Sunday paper, said,

"I fucking believe nothing now."

The Church had laid down a decree that details of payouts to victims, the crimes of the perpetrators, would be sealed for—wait for it—

Seventy-five years.

You had to shout,

"How are they getting away with this shite?"

A guy sitting on my right kept sneaking looks at me. At first I didn't take too much notice but then it began to snip at my nerves. I asked,

"Help you with something?"

He had a shifty air about him, like he knew where your wallet was and, worse, where it was headed. He said,

"I know you, just can't quite place it."

There are times you sit easily in a pub, the TV is off and all you hear are the muted conversations; something comforting about it. You're only half aware of your surroundings but it's peaceful. As you tune in and out of the chat. That was now pretty much fucked.

Then he lit up, said,

"You're that guy, the miracle fellah. A truck walloped you and those kids brought you back to life."

Lord above, how stories get embellished. I hadn't the energy to tell him the facts but he was far from done, he said,

"So, if I touch you, I'll be like blessed."

I turned round to full face him, said,

"You touch me, blessed is the very last thing you'll be."

If you ever walk past a nun
Immediately
Touch a piece of iron
Or say
"*Your nun*"
To a passerby
Passing
The bad luck
To them.

(Italian superstition)

Connie still considered herself a nun but whether official religions would recognize her as such was open to debate. Back in her days as a prison chaplain, she had viewed nuns as basically lesser than her own profession but being stripped of her chaplainship had cut deep. Sure, she had violated some rules of the correctional facility, but she felt they overreacted by insisting she not be sacked but relieved of her profession.

She felt it was humility to reinvent herself as a nun—plus the scrutiny was less rigorous. You had to love California; you were a nun if you said so.

Now, she was deep in the affair with Benjamin J. Cullen. Piece by slow piece he had revealed his hobby.

Arson.

Shocked? She was less horrified than she might have expected. You had a man who treated you like a queen. So what if he indulged in a little mischief.

Brid. Ah, Brid, becoming more and more of a problem, whining on an hourly basis.

Benjamin disappeared frequently, on business he said, offering,

"How else can I continue to treat you like a princess, huh?"

He'd come back from a trip to France. If you'll excuse the dreadful pun, he was all lit up, said to her in a tone of huge excitement,

"Damn near achieved a masterpiece."

She'd no idea what he was on about. He said,
"Turn on the TV."
She did.
Notre-Dame was on fire.

One of the investigators of the Notre-Dame fire, a veteran of global infernos, had once worked with Red Adair. The official verdict was, perhaps, an electrical spark. This investigator, named O'Rourke, decided to walk the surrounding perimeter and stopped as he noticed a small bundle of long-stem matches, picked one up, saw it was the nonsafety kind, pondered it for a moment, then shrugged, dropped the match, moved on.

Ireland was in shock; a young journalist, Lyra, aged twenty-eight, covering an event, was shot dead. Huge crowds turned out declaring they would not tolerate a return to the old days of violence.

I was watching a documentary titled *Moving Statues: The Summer of 1985*.

For fifteen mad weeks, the country was gripped by reports of life-size statues that moved, wobbled, wept, and swayed. Small villages, reporting a movement of Our Lady, would suddenly be engulfed by up to twenty thousand pilgrims, then a sighting in another village and the crowds moved on. Perhaps the most telling aspect of all this was the Church's reaction: condemned it as manipulating the most vulnerable of the people. That, of course, was its province. Not to mention that the official shrines, the real money earners like Knock, might have a dip in revenue.

Mass hysteria was cited as the cause and one bishop termed it *contagion*.

The current miracle in Galway hadn't really mushroomed. The absence of the children was one factor and the crowds began to fall off.

No matter all my inquires I hadn't found the children; they seemed to have vanished. Monsignor Rael, the Vatican guy sent to quell the phenomenon, came to see me. He appeared to be well pleased the whole matter had evaporated.

He was in my apartment, looking with slight distaste at the lack of furnishings, asked,

"Is this just a temporary home?"

I didn't like him any better than the first time I'd met him. I said,

"Surely all of our existence is temporary."

He didn't rise to the bait, said,

"The fee we gave you?"

Waited.

I said nothing. He continued,

"Let's call it a retainer: We may need your irregular services in the future."

I asked,

"You're done with the miracle, that's it, end of story?"

He smiled, a very ancient one, framed from decades of Vatican chicanery, said,

"It was never really going anywhere but best to nip it in the bud."

I pushed.

"The welfare of the children, that doesn't concern you, even a little?"

The smile mutated into something more sinister. He said,

"When and if they show up we shall of course be very attentive."

Then he changed direction, rubbed his finely manicured hands, said,

"Let's have a wee drink to mark the end of this whole sorry episode. You do have libations, I'm sure. I mean, it's what you do after all, drink?"

My turn, I snarled,

"Not if your life depended on it."

He actually made that *tut-tut* sound that grinds my nerves, said,

"How small-minded of you, Taylor, but everything in your small world is thus. Tiny gestures masquerading as victories."

Something occurred to me and I said,

"Malachy, I imagine he's not about to be our next bishop?"

Now he laughed outright, sneered,

"That imbecile was never in the frame, good heavens, he's the worst kind of PR."

I really wanted to batter him into humility but that would be pretty much a lost cause. I said,

"You need to go now."

He took a last look around, said,

"If I cared at all, I might even pity you."

I opened the door, wanting to be shot of him and his maliciousness.

I said,

"The terrible thing is, there are some decent priests around. I've even met one or two, but you, you're more than likely the new face of the future, the slick corporate asshole who never leaves prints."

He was delighted at this, said,

"For a moment there, Taylor, you verged on actual insight. I doubt we'll meet again but it's been entertaining."

Not sure if I even thought about it as my hand lashed out and slapped his face, twice, hard and fierce.

He was stunned, took a moment to focus, then warned,

"You'll regret that."

I finally got to smile, said,

"My whole life is a tapestry of regret but I promise you that will never, ever be something to add to the list."

For the first time, in a very long time, I felt a tiny touch of pride in my own self.

A
  MIRACLE
      ENGULFED
           OBLITERATED
           DECIMATED
                  IN
                       FIRE

Benjamin J. was outlining the plan to Connie. Almost every aspect of it horrified her. He registered her reluctance, demanded,

"Who said those children had to die to make this miracle unique? Wasn't that your idea?"

She didn't answer, lost in the part where Brid had to die. He moved in front of her and, with slow measured timing, slapped her face, harsh enough to leave the track of his fingers on her cheek. He snarled,

"Either get with the game or wallow in obscurity. You want to burn with glory or be like that parasite Brid, a feeble thing that pisses and moans."

She managed to pull herself together, said,

"I'm in."

He gave her a second slap, keep the vibe alive as it were. Then,

"Here's what we're going to do. You and Brid go in the house. I'll have dealt with the children and their minder, so no problem there. The timers will kick in and you simply need to ensure your ally joins the martyrs."

He seemed to relish the word *martyrs*, continued,

"Then you stagger outside, your arm badly burned, collapse beautifully for your photo opportunity, wail, *oh I tried to save them*. The media will lap it up. Then you can swoon or whatever you deem appropriate."

He paused, asked,

"You can do hysteria, right?"

She could barely think but said,

"I'm hysterical already."

He raised his hand, warned,

"Save it. We don't want to appear rehearsed."

He moved to the drink cabinet, plucked out a bottle of Black Bushmills, said,

"Let's have a wee dram to cement our grand design."

Her mind was already in flames and a moment of insane logic had her ask,

"Isn't Bushmills the Protestant drink?"

The best laid plans.

Connie moved through the smoking house, flames everywhere. Brid had gone upstairs to deal with the children and the carer. To her astonishment, she found one child dead, his throat cut, and the carer bedside him, also dead. No sign of the other child. She rushed down to tell Connie, who walloped her with the tire iron.

Connie hit her again, screaming,

"I'm so sorry!"

The fire was in full rage, she whispered,

"Another minute and I'm out of here."

She did as Benjamin had instructed and put out her hand, let the fire travel up to her shoulder. The pain was beyond belief and she quickly managed to douse it but the agony . . . She could hardly see, made her way to the door, pulled the handle.

Locked.

How the fuck could that be?

She turned to see the fire speeding toward her, pulled frantically at the door, then realized, as the flames reached her, that Benjamin had locked her in.

Her last words were

"Oh, Brid."

The fire took her.

It took two battalions of firefighters nearly five hours before the blaze could be contained. A fire inspector, hours later, on his first cursory inspection, hung his head in shock, said to his deputy,

"Multiple casualties, including a child."

The deputy said,

"Sweet Jesus."

Benjamin J. watching the inferno from a safe distance, laid out five nonsafety matches, said,

"One each."

He prided himself on his expertise with figures, never got them wrong.

He did now.

His count of five was wrong.

It was four.

* * *

The fire and resultant deaths did not play large in the media, as you would have expected. Almost immediately it was suppressed, with a report saying,

"Tragic accident involving members of a religious community."

No one wanted to stir up what might be a fiasco, with the death of the miracle child, a highly suspicious fire, the death of two American nuns. The term "ongoing investigation" successfully quelled awkward questions.

The miracle of Galway was officially dead.

I met with Owen Daglish, bought him the obligatory drinks, and let him talk. He seemed as shocked as anyone else, began with,

"It's a clusterfuck of epic size."

I waited.

Then,

"The two dodgy nuns, Yanks, only added to the potential scandal so it is felt that the whole shebang is best left alone."

I asked,

"And the child? Where is the other one?"

He shrugged, said,

"Collateral damage, but the Church seems relieved the whole miracle business is over."

I pushed,

"What about arson?"

He rounded on me, literally put a hand to my mouth, warned,

"Shush. Jesus, don't even breathe the word."

He drank a double Jameson in a gulp, said,

"The Guards would be in deep shit if arson had occurred, especially as it was suspected for some time that other dodgy fires were never fully investigated."

I sneered,

"Case closed."

He had no answer so I ventured,

"Ever hear of Benjamin J. Cullen?"

I could tell by his face that he had. He looked away, then said,

"No."

I said,

"You're a bad liar."

That gem hovered over for us until he said,

"Cullen was of interest to us but he's connected to all kinds of top people so we were told to stay away from him."

I said,

"He gave me a nonsafety match: It's his calling card."

Owen sighed, said,

"A discreet investigation was conducted but nothing solid was found. The guy gives out matches. Try bringing that to a judge—a judge Cullen plays golf with."

I stood up. Owen asked,

"You don't want another round?"

I tried to keep my rage in check, said,

"I'd love another drink."

He seemed relieved, said,

"There you go, same again?"

I said,

"Just not with you."

I got back to my apartment late. Shadows in the hallway and what appeared to be a bundle of rags outside my door. I edged forward cautiously. In the past, items left outside my door brought nothing but strife and violence.

The bundle moved. A small face appeared.

I was dumbstruck.

The girl Sara, one of the miracle children. She looked at me, said,

"Help me."

I got her inside, gave her tea, biscuits, all of which she devoured with a fierce focus. I waited until she settled a bit, then I asked,

"How?"

I expected her to speak, if she could indeed speak at all, in broken English, but her English was near fluent—just one of many surprises to come. She said,

"I have listened and imitated English for many years, all the time of my travel."

Then,

"May I have more tea?"

I got that, my mind in wonder mode, poured a large Jay for my own self. She said,

"I followed you after you got out of the hospital. I believed there was something on your face that said you were a man who helps."

I said,

"You're very grown-up for what? Fourteen years of age?"

She gave a tiny smile and it transformed her from urchin to someone aware and capable.

She said,

"I am much more in years than that but, during our travels, our being moved from country to country, it was wise to seem like a child."

The question hanging over us,

The fire?

She saw in my face, said,

"I was not in the house."

I asked the glaring question,

"Why?"

She studied my face, found nothing to spook her, said,

"I go to get candies for the boy. 'Candies' is the correct word?"

The fuck I knew but I nodded.

Her face crumpled for a moment and a tiny tear escaped, rolled down her cheek, fell to the carpet with—I swear—a soft sound. She composed herself with a practiced effort, fixed her features into a hard nine-yard stare, said,

"I cannot say his name, not since he burned, and I had left him unsafe, always, before, in all the danger, the ships, the bad men . . ."

Paused.

"The very bad men, women too, I kept *my boys* safe. I had a knife after Greece, and I used it."

A hint of pride in that but short-lived as she realized again she wasn't there when it counted. She continued,

"I saw the man."

Fuck.

I held up a hand, went,

"Whoa, what man?"

Her face darkened, she spat,

"The man who set the fire, the man who waited until it burned high, then he bolted—is right word, to 'bolt'? To stop? The door?"

God almighty.

I checked,

"You saw him? You saw him clearly?"

She looked at me, asked,

"You see the demon, you think maybe you forget what he looks like?"

I poured another Jay, she asked,

"This is Irish whiskey?"

I held the bottle mid-pour, asked,

"You know it?"

She gave a mirthless laugh, said,

"I know

Brandy.

Ouzo.

Metaxa.

Tequila.

Rake.

On the ships, all the travels, the men, they give us all kinds of drinks, to have a way with us?"

Jesus. I didn't want to ask. Would you?

She said,

"I had my knife and I drank their poisons."

Added sadly,

"The boy, they made him sick so I drank his."

My face must have registered some of my horror. She said,

"I tell you before, I tell you, I am older than my face. My body is small, no food or food with worms, you do not develop, but my mind, I fed my mind with hate. Hate makes you old in the heart, in the soul."

Unconsciously, I muttered,

"An old soul."

She gave me a lovely smile and it transformed this girl-child into something glorious, something fantastically ferocious in the very best way.

She put her hand out, commanded,

"Now give me Irish whiskey where I do not have to use my knife."

There was absolute threat in this request but a soft pleading too. I poured her a shot, she held the glass still outstretched, said,

"A drink for not-a-child."

I poured more and she drank it like a docker.

I asked,

"You were there when a truck hit me."

She gave a guilty smile, so I pushed,

"Did you try to rob me?"

"Yes."

I near shouted,

"You could try denying it, for God's sake."

She went hard-core serious.

"I do not lie. I do many things that are very not good but I never lie."

Oddly, I believed her.

Another smile, then,

"I know a man who is good—dangerous but good. I know because in the three years of our journeys to this . . ."

Pause.

". . . place, I have known almost nothing but the terrible men, so one who has some soul of light, I know it."

Well, I was this far in, might as well go for broke. I asked,

"The miracle? The Madonna cry, what was that."

Without a beat, she said,

"A trick, a cheap light trick they have in village in Guatemala."

Before I could echo "Guatemala," she yawned, asked,

"Please, now I sleep."

I gave her my bed, said,

"Sleep well. You are safe here."

She gave me an impish grin, said,

"Of course. I have my knife."

Touché.

As she turned to go, I noticed the snake tattoo on her left arm. As her arm stretched out, it seemed as if the snake, a cobra, unfurled, its hood in full effect, the fangs clearly etched, and, I swear to god, it looked like it was about to strike me. I jumped back in fright, muttered,

"Fuck, get a grip."

She smiled and almost absentmindedly scratched at what appeared to be a cross under her left jaw.

She then uttered a sentence I didn't understand. The way she said it, it sounded like a curse. I am far too familiar with curses to mistake one for a blessing. She then gave me a look of such sultry, sensual intensity that I had to turn away. She disappeared into the bedroom. I was badly shaken, got a pen, and wrote down what she'd said as phonetically as I was able.

Took me ten minutes to find an approximation on Google; it was Aramaic.

Another ten minutes to attempt a translation; it seemed to be:

You will perish in awesome torment.

No, that couldn't be right. She was just a young, traumatized child, and I would keep her safe. Like all my bright ideas, interpretations, I was utterly wrong.

I sat by her bed, keeping vigil.

Alas, being a semiliterate horror movie buff, the movies

Orphan.

Case 39.

Did cross my mind.

Both feature a child way older than appearances suggest.

I shrugged them off, or tried to. Then Sara began to shiver, soundlessly scream, make contorted turns in the bed. Sweat was rolling in rivulets off her tiny form. Warily, I got a damp cloth, tried to cool her brow, all the while aware she might suddenly knife me.

A leaflet slipped out from under her pillow. It had a picture of a small village, Ballyfin, and a plea to save the village. The headline was simple:

"Provide Our Miracle."

I'd work that out later. Right now, I needed another opinion.

I phoned Keefer, said I needed his help.

He didn't ask why or when, simply said,

"You got it."

Such friends are utter gold.

"When
I
Was
Five
I
Was
Just
Alive"

(A. A. Milne, *Now We Are Six*)

Keefer and I were in my living room, sipping brewed coffee—not instant, yer actual roasted beans, whole real nine-yards gig. Keefer felt it was his influence as, on a previous occasion, I had given him a mug of instant that he unceremoniously spat on my not-so-new rug, snarled,

"What is this shit?"

Now, he was here, satisfied with the real java (Colombian, if you persist), dressed per usual like a cross between biker/thug/longshoreman. His bike boots were perched on the coffee table due not so much to horrendous manners but to the spliff he'd just smoked. I'd been all righteous, saying,

"Little early for recreational drugs."

Got the withering look, then he produced his silver flask with the Stones tongue logo, a flask that on close scrutiny had what seemed like bullet dents in it.

"Altamont,"

He said.

When I asked.

He unscrewed the top, poured some liquid into my mug of still-steaming coffee, said,

"Kentucky sour mash."

Tasted real fine.

Took a full pot of the elite coffee for me to lay out the whole saga of the miracle girl and why she was now sleeping in my apartment. He took it all in, then,

"Fuck."

I said,

"Might need a little more than that, buddy."

He looked at me, said,

"You have an uncanny knack of attracting the weirdest vibes. You know that, right?"

I said,

"She can identify the man who not only set the fire but bolted the front door to prevent anyone from getting out."

The horror of it touched his eyes, which first turned a shade of sadness I had rarely seen, then he shook himself and his eyes returned to the dark slate he presented to the outside. He guessed,

"You're thinking this is our old buddy Benjamin J., the non-safety match dude?"

I noticed a worn paperback protruding from his side pocket, went,

"You're reading?"

Alas, my tone did carry a hint of superciliousness that only a complete asshole would do. He pulled it out, ignoring my barb, said,

"Hey, you're the guy who told me to read some mystery novels. You said, I think, some of the best writing is in that neighborhood these days."

He handed over the book, battered as it was:

Tin Roof Blowdown,

By James Lee Burke.

I said,

"It's a stone-cold classic and disproves the idea that a series goes stale. This, his sixteenth, is his best ever and probably the finest writing on Katrina."

God only knows how long I would have droned on about American mystery writers but the bedroom door opened and Sara came out, wearing an old Notre Dame sweatshirt that Emerald had left behind.

If you were a literary type, you might suggest a Kate Atkinson use of coincidence between the shirt and the fire in Paris the week before.

She held a small book in her hand, asked, sleep in her voice,

"Who is A. A. Milne?"

She saw the leaflet on Ballyfin on the table, snapped it away, warned,

"Do not put your nose in my business, ever."

She sounded like a complete psycho, like the cobra about to strike, her lethalness uncoiling like a black slither. Keefer didn't even notice. I blame that fucking whiskey.

She took a step back when she saw Keefer, her body in flight/fight mode. She asked,

"Who is he?"

Keefer gave a warm smile, a rare to rarer event for him, said,

"I'm the dude who brought breakfast."

Reached in his backpack, produced cornflakes, pancakes, asked,

"You think Jack has breakfast stuff?"

She shook her head. Keefer stood, handed me the items, said,

"Go be domestic."

I managed to produce some bowls, heated the pancakes, made tea, more coffee, put this hopeful bunch on the table. Keefer looked at Sara, asked,

"What's missing?"

Before I could say,

Her childhood.

He said,

"Can't have no pancakes without syrup, am I right, girl?"

Put up his palm and, fuck me, she high-fived him.

How'd that happen?

When she'd finished, I suggested,

"Sara can give us a description of the man who set the fire."

I turned to her, said,

"Now take your time, think carefully, and tell anything you can recall of what he looked like."

Keefer made a sound of disgust, said,

"No need to waste time. Let's cut to the chase."

We both looked at him in dismay. I said,

"What are you thinking?"

He produced a shiny iPhone and handled it like it was his go-to accessory. He'd sworn a line through hell would happen before he'd be caught with such an item. I said,

"You hate phones."

He gave me a look of bafflement, went,

"Me? Dude, you got to have one."

Many things were annoying about that answer, starting with *dude*, but I let them slide, waited. He asked, pulling up a photo on his screen,

"This guy?"

Sara physically shrank from the image, nodded her head. He turned the phone to me. There was Benjamin J.

I was impressed, asked,

"How'd you get that?"

He smirked, like I was being deliberately dense, said slowly,

"I put the phone in his face, clicked."

It was an answer.

Sara was curled up in the chair. I went to her but Keefer caught my arm, said,

"I got this."

He knelt down and spoke in a low, near whisper to her. For minutes she didn't respond, then she uncurled, a tiny smile at the corner of her mouth. He said,

"You go get washed up, hon."

She didn't dance away but she was for sure much better. I asked,

"What did you tell her?"

He said,

"I told her the truth."

Fuck.

"Mind sharing that?"

He made a face of *Lord grant me patience with this idiot*, said,

"I told her we'd kill the fucker."

>   *My daughter's dead clothes.*

Or

>   *My dead daughter's clothes.*

After the death of my daughter, those two sentences bounced, danced, and mired in my mind. I was so consumed with madness, grief, anger that those lines were like a cursed mantra in my head. Round and round they spun in an insane reel. Fueled with Jameson, I was fixated on which was the correct statement.

I'd even gone to church, sought out a priest, and laid that question on him. I scared the shit out of him. He didn't actually flee but he backed away fast, muttering,

"Perhaps some medical help?"

The day before her death, I had bought her jeans, sweatshirts, the small Converse trainers she loved, and wrapped them with great care. Men can't fold a parcel for shit but I tried and figured if I put a bow on it, it would be less of a befuddled mess.

That care/less package had lain at the bottom of my wardrobe ever since, untouched, unseen. I told Keefer that the clothes might fit Sara; I couldn't meet his eyes as I did so.

He asked,

"You sure, buddy? I can go out, get some gear."

I managed,

"No, it's fine."

It wasn't fine, it would never be fucking fine. Never.

I had some very bad dreams in the days after Sara left. I woke one night and wrote down a thought, then went back to sleep.

In the morning, I read this:

> *"You search in a black dark cave for a candle*
> *That was lit*
> *Two thousand years ago."*

Benjamin J. didn't fuck up.

That was as close to a slogan as he'd ever come.

He'd fucked up.

One of the miracle children had survived the inferno.

He replayed the days before the fire.

He'd mounted a massive charm campaign on Brid to persuade her to lead the way into the house they'd burn. Took some doing but his full attention and flattery did the trick and she actually said to Connie,

"I may have been wrong about him."

He'd laid out the details to Connie.

"You and Brid go in, chloroform the children and their carer, then you . . ."

Pause.

"Disable Brid, allow your arm to be burned, and flee."

He gave Connie the gasoline, said,

"Spread freely."

She was very dubious but he bamboozled her with an engagement ring, said,

"Not only will you be a hero, nearly a martyr, hurt as you tried to save the children and your best friend, but you will soon be Mrs. Benjamin J."

He'd rehearsed the two women at different times, drilled them on the importance of fine timing. He was well pleased with his machinations, fooling one woman is not so difficult but two, simultaneously, it was a friggin' work of art.

The actual day of the fire, it seemed to be proceeding to plan, and as soon as he saw the first signs of the flames, he rushed to the door, bolted it, and whispered,

"Good-bye my love, good-bye."

If he had waited for a moment, he might have heard Connie scream.

Might have heard her scream,

"One of the children is missing."

Benjamin J. was seriously pissed. How could Connie have missed out on one child? A survivor was very bad news. If Connie were still alive, he'd have flayed her, shouted,

"You dumb bitch."

Where was the child now? Had she seen him?

He was at home. Home was what he termed *a rather splendid mansion* off Threadneedle Road. The name of the road amused him in foolish ways. Three stories high, with huge bay windows, a small courtyard leading to the main door—and what a door, made of reenforced steel, covered in timber, it proclaimed,

"Here lives a person of note."

The furniture was Scandinavian, all clean lines. His pride of joy were framed paintings of historical fires. He could stare at them, lost for hours in their splendor. In a separate glass case was a collection of matches from different decades in history.

He paced back and forth in his massive living room, raging at the debacle of the recent fire. When he was thwarted in any of his endeavors, his usual solution was to burn something. But caution urged he stay under the radar for a time, see what developed.

He thought about Connie and a warm feeling ran through him. It had been a total rush to fuck with her head. Her sidekick had been too feeble a creature to afford him any real joy. He wished he could have seen Connie's face when she realized he had set her up.

"Ah . . ."

He thought.

"The joy of betrayal."

In an effort to calm his mind, he worked on the latest set of accounts he'd been commissioned to fix for a major firm. A cursory glance told him how easy it would be to settle the books to satisfy the most diligent of audits. He would of course delay his findings until the last moment, let them sweat, then swoop in, save the day.

For a hefty fee.

Benjamin J. studied his face in the mirror. What he saw was a face of refinery and breeding. A very carefully constructed facade, years in the making.

On most humans it worked, lulled them into the artifice. See the gig with the late Connie, for example. He'd studied the tomes of

Psychology.

Pathology.

Origins of evil.

People of the lie.

Even amused himself with the psychopath test and, yes, he was off the chart on that baby. Years of immersion in the realms of malignity were hugely beneficial to his means of not only surviving in the world but flourishing. He discovered early that arson was his fuel, so to speak.

Fire.

How he worshipped it.

It vaguely amused him that the classic early signs of a killer/psychopath didn't apply to him. He hadn't set fires in his youth, tortured animals, been a loner, endured abuse as a child. All of this supplied his answer.

He was simply *other*.

Hate.

Hate suffused him, lit him up, and, even better, he could present as what the masses termed *a people person*.

This term was among his absolute favorites.

He studied arson with the zeal of a devotee. How to set the perfect infernos that, to date, were labeled accidental. A tribute to his years of research.

He had perfected timers that, after they ignited, self-destructed.

Took years to get that utterly undetectable; his flames devoured everything.

Until now.

A witness.

Sent a shudder of an unexpected feeling.

Fear.

But he shook it off. He was *the arsonist*. He'd successfully set a series of fires and not one visit from the Guards. How magnificent was that!

Now it was time to recruit a patsy. Connie had been a blast, dare one hazard, that for a short time had lit his fire but onward and fireward. Nothing finer than to groom some dumb schmuck, set them up, let them believe they actually mattered, then lower the boom. Plus, they were useful for errands. I mean, was he expected to, like, collect his own dry cleaning?

Get real.

Too, at a certain stage, he did enjoy the fawning, the admiration.

And, let's face it, if you wanted a fuck-up in waiting, an actual dope, then Galway was a sea of infinite choices.

The Unit.

The psychiatric wing of the general hospital, all sorts of mental blitzkrieg to choose from, be it

Anorexics.

Junkies.

Depressives.

Alcoholics.

Oh, Lord, a panorama of twenty-first-century casualties and growing every day.

Benjamin J. belonged to a group of prominent businessmen, professionals who devoted time and especially funds to help patients on their release. It worked nicely, too, as a tax write-off.

Benjamin had already selected his candidate.

James Powell, twenty-six years old, victim of serial abuse, addicted to solvents, and due for release on a heavy dosage of meds. Benjamin had already visited with the poor lad and was well en route to gaining his trust.

James would suit his plans perfectly.

"The Tecate is ice cold and a storm is rolling across the desert. The rain's musky fragrance rides the blast-furnace wind as a jukebox grinds on in a cantina's corner."

(Freddy Fender crooning "Across the Borderline")

A thousand footprints in the sand . . . reveal the secret no one can define.

(Craig McDonald)

Keefer suggested that Sara hide out at his farm until we dealt with Benjamin J. He looked kind of bashful as he added,

"I, um, have somebody there at the moment."

This was news. I pushed,

"Yeah, you didn't think to mention that? Who is it?"

He didn't meet my eyes, said,

"Ceola. She came to attend to the horses, and, um, then turned out she's a massive Stones fan."

He trailed off.

God forgive me but I was getting a kick out of baiting him, accused,

"Remember the rules you laid down for me, *no stories, no anecdotes about the Stones*. Different deal if it's a woman. That's almost gender bias there, pal."

He was packing a small holdall for Sara, said,

"Good for Ramona to have a woman around."

Watching his face, I thought,

"Oh, hello!"

Asked,

"What age are she and Ceola? Never heard that name."

Sensing a mild diversion, he followed,

"Ceola. It's Gaelic for music, or melody, so you know, with my life with music, it seemed meant to be, you think?"

Undeterred, I asked,

"Age?"

Again, he was uncomfortable, tried,

"Age. Too much is made of age. I mean, if two people like each other . . . ?"

I was having a high old time, guessed,

"So, young?"

"Youngish."

Now I laughed, said,

"Great Stones legacy, eh? Young chicks for old farts."

He looked hurt, which was rare. I'd seen him beaten by thugs, saddened by death, but this particular hurt, no. He said,

"Even for you, Jack, that's a low blow."

And it was.

Not for the first time, I wondered, *The fuck was wrong with me?* People who were close to me, had been close to me, sooner or later, I drove them from me. I tried,

"Come on, buddy, I'm just fucking with you."

He asked,

"Are there not enough shitheels out in the world for you to vent on, you have to bring it home?"

I was saved from answering, Sara appearing with her rucksack packed. She asked,

"Are you fighting?"

I was ready with a platitude but Keefer got there first, said,

"Our friend here, he can be a real nasty piece of work sometimes."

Sara allowed herself a small smile, said,
"I know."

After they left, I felt a mix of grief, regret, guilt.

Grief for the little girl Sara, seemingly tossed on the waves of a world that could care less.

Regret for the nasty words I'd laid on Keefer.

Guilt, for every damn thing.

The day before, I'd gone to an ATM, taken out a few hundred euros to help with the goods Sara would need but, in the bad vibe of them leaving, I forgot.

Went to get my wallet, maybe I could catch them up, took my jacket from the bedroom. The wallet.

Empty.

Not a fucking note left.

Worse, a gold miraculous medal that had belonged to my daughter that was folded in a small secure pocket of the wallet, it was gone too.

Sara.

The thief.

The thief who knew Aramaic.

Thing is, I had a sort of sneaking admiration for her.

How fucked is that?

I should have phoned later, maybe told Keefer, but I wasn't sure he would react too well to me calling a young girl a thief, especially after I'd flat out insulted him already.

So I didn't.

Didn't call.

One lethal error of judgment that would inform all that was to come.

Later in the day, I watched as Theresa May finally resigned, after three years of fuckhawking with Europe. It was now the time of true idiocy as Farage seemed likely to ascend to power. Another fool, the dangerous braggart Boris Johnson, vied for leadership of the Tories.

Johnson, like his eerie twin Trump, was born in New York.

Odd thing, if you looked at the initials of the deadly three, it was almost uncanny.

Donald Trump. D.T. Delirium Tremens.

Boris Johnson. B.J. Which was pretty much self-explanatory.

Nigel Farage. F.T. The National Front.

The country was in the grip of *claim fever*.

The slightest of what were once simple accidents in the course of life were now cause for legal recourse and payouts. Reached a crescendo when a member of the government claimed a fall from a swing in a fashionable hotel was grounds for a major claim. That she managed to run a 10 km race two weeks after the fall didn't help her creditability. The media had a riot of coverage, and celebrities of every hue were photographed on swings *without injury*.

Amid a storm of outrage she withdrew her claim but her image was forever linked to that swing.

A former Rose of Tralee, who was the first gay Rose, decided to run for a seat in Europe despite having no political experience. Someone, someday, would look back and ask reasonably,

"What the fuck happened to Ireland?"

I was catching up on the local papers, reading Kernan Andrews in the *Galway Advertiser*. He was reporting on the suicide/drowning of a local man. Something nagged at me. I read further. The man had recently lost his wife and son and, at one stage, had been a *person of interest* in the deaths of his family.

Fuck, wait a minute.

Keefer had stressed we had three cases.

The miracle children.

The troll case.

And.

The one he took over, the guy who might have thrown his wife through a window, the woman who had come to me begging for help against her husband. The guy had an alibi but Keefer was convinced he had killed his wife and their child. Keefer had met with him, told me,

"The scumbag is guilty as hell."

I had said that there was little we could do if he was alibied. Now I remember Keefer saying,

"Well, nothing legal can be done."

I'd shrugged it away.

I muttered to myself,

"He wouldn't, no, no way. He wouldn't go off on his own bat, take action, and not tell me?"

I called him, laid out what I'd read in the papers. He was silent, then,

"I heard when he was pulled from the water he was wearing a T-shirt."

What? So what?

Keefer gave what sounded like a nasty chuckle, said,

"It's what they say the logo on the T-shirt was."

I was afraid to ask, as I had a bad feeling it wasn't going to ease my dread. I asked,

"Yeah, what was that?"

A pause.

Then,

"Life."

Took me a minute, then,

"Oh my God, that's the name of Keith Richards's memoir."

I could hear him chuckle. He said,

"I'm impressed. You have learned your Stones lore very well."

There was silence, the implication writ large, then I asked,

"That would suggest you might have had some involvement in his demise."

He laughed outright, said,

"You sound like a frigging lawyer. Spit it out, pilgrim. The bad cunt was murdered."

I said nothing. I was dumbfounded, so he added,

"Aren't you the hardass who said the law was for courts, justice was in the alley?"

I managed,

"But murder?"

Now his tone changed. He said,

"What would you do, carve his initials in his desk?"

That landed.

How he knew that was how I'd dealt with the troll was a whole other question.

At a loss, I said,

"I need to think about this."

He said,

"See it this way. The Keith Richards reference: You might say I was writing my own story."

I said,

"I better go."

Heard a sharp intake of breath, then he snarled,

"You're not going to ask?"

"What?"

I near shouted.

He said,

"One would have thought you might ask after the girl, or even the falcon."

Then he clicked off.

My mind was seriously fucked. I poured a Jameson, swallowed it fast, wished I had some Xanax, wished I had some other life. Then the doorbell went. I tried to think of anyone I'd be glad to see. Nope, not a one.

Opened the door to Malachy.

He looked like my mind felt.

Wretched.

When he'd been bishop-elect, he'd cleaned up good, stopped smoking, had a haircut, wore crisp new attire, but that was all in the clerical wind. He stormed in, muttered,

"I need a drink."

I stared at him: a rumpled suit, the white collar of the priest-hood askew, his hair like a small jungle and dandruff on his shoulders, his eyes bloodshot, his face a riot of blotches.

I poured him a Jay. He looked at the measure, snapped,

"Are you rationing it?"

I added more. Did he say "thank you"?

Right.

He gulped the drink, burped, seemed like he might throw up but the drink took him another direction, into some realm of almost calm, artificial as it was.

He lit a cigarette, blew billows of smoke, said,

"I'd have been a great bishop."

He was the essence of despair. I tried,

"They'll probably give you something to compensate."

I didn't believe that for a moment. He snarled,

"They will like fuck."

I asked,

"Don't suppose you could sue?"

Enraged him. He spat,

"Sue the Church. See how far the child abuse victims got with that."

True.

Then he straightened up, like a plan was evolving. That usually involved me doing something for him that I really didn't want to. He said,

"There's talk one of the miracle children survived the fire."

Aw, fuck. I knew where this was headed. I said,

"No."

He attempted to form his face into an expression of pleading but it didn't quite take. It was more a grimace. He whined,

"If I were to deliver that child, they might reconsider me for bishop."

I was split between outrage and incredulity, asked,

"Deliver?"

I had to choke down rising bile, continued,

"*Deliver* from what, *deliver us from evil?* You'd give her to the Church and they have such a record of virtue with children."

He was on his feet, frustrated, said,

"I'd be a good bishop."

I laughed, said,

"*Good* and *bishop* just don't fit in the same sentence, and you'd be a shite bishop."

He reached out a hand. I thought he was going to grab me but he clocked my face, let his hand fall back, and pleaded,

"You owe me, Taylor."

This was too ridiculous even to argue. I said,

"I'll make a deal with you. If you care about this child, tell me her name."

Confounded him but he rallied, said,

"That's madness, of course I know her name."

I said,

"So tell me."

He raised his eyes to heaven but I don't think he found any solace there. He said,

"Theresa?"

In the mid-nineteenth century
Pyromania was considered to be
A morbid propensity to incendiarism
Where the mind,
Though otherwise sound,
Is borne on by an invisible power
To the commission of this crime
That is now recognized
As a distinct form of insanity

(Chloe Hooper, *The Arsonist*)

Time to go shake up the arsonist. Google Maps showed his house just off Threadneedle Road; this was an area that never could decide if it was

A. Part of the elite of Taylor's Hill

Or

B. The shady environs of Salthill.

Benjamin J.'s house was impressive, one of those new mock Georgian piles that exuded money, if not class. Solar panels on the roof to showcase green credentials made me think of the recent European elections. The Green Party won big, Sinn Féin, not so much. A wit said they could unite to be

"Guns and Roses."

A vintage Bentley in the driveway. I knocked on the door, waited. Opened by a young man wearing a boiler suit, like a would-be mechanic. He had blond hair, soft features, one of those moon faces that echoed steroids. His eyes were askew so that though he looked at you, it was as if he were seeing something in his peripheral vision. I figured some heavy drug dosage had scrambled his brain. He asked,

"Yes?"

I said,

"I'm here to see Mr. Cullen."

This seemed to confuse him, so I added,

"Benjamin J."

He considered this, asked,

"What's the 'J' for?"

I guessed,

"Jerusalem?"

His face lit up. He asked,

"Really?"

God only knows how long this inane chat would have meandered on.

Benjamin J. appeared behind the man, touched him on the shoulder, said,

"James, go and see to the dogs."

James looked at him, confusion writ large, said,

"We don't have dogs."

Benjamin gave a tight smile, snarled,

"Clean up the kitchen. Just go."

Reluctantly, he did.

Benjamin managed to rein in his annoyance, asked,

"Mr. Taylor, how may we be of service?"

I said,

"A wee chat would be good."

His mouth curled up at the idea. He said,

"Perhaps you might ring, make an appointment."

I stepped toward him, said,

"It's about fire insurance."

He faltered but only briefly, made a show of looking at his watch, a Rolex, said,

"We can manage that."

I followed him inside to a living room lined with books, the type of books for show, not tell, a large oil painting over the fireplace, and, no surprise, *The Great Fire of London*.

I said,

"Bit obvious that, no?"

He smiled, gave it a long appraisal, said,

"One of the greats, the pinnacle we might all aspire too."

I said,

"For psychos, I'm sure."

He frowned, as if seriously disappointed, said,

"I expected better of you, Jack. May I call you 'Jack'?"

I gave him a look, asked,

"If I call you 'Benny'?"

He did a twirl on his heels, turned to a drinks cabinet, said,

"I'm going to change the energy of this whole meeting. I feel a certain hostility from you so, to start over, let me fix you a drink. Jameson work?"

He poured two fine measures, handed me one, then moved to a high-back chair, said,

"Chin-chin."

I thought,

Like people actually say this shit?

I was about to speak when he held up a finger, said,

"One moment before we get to what I feel will be unpleasant. Let me ask you two pertinent questions."

Somehow, he had gained the upper hand in this sparring but I could run with it for a bit, said,

"*Fire* away."

Got a brief bitter smile for my pun, then he asked,

"Your biker friend, the Rolling Stones chap, does he still have his farm outside of town?"

Letting me know he knew where Keefer lived. I said,

"Yeah."

He mulled that over, then,

"Good, that's excellent. Now the second question is . . ."

Paused.

"Have you ever watched a sheep burn?"

I let out a deep breath, asked,

"Are you threatening me?"

He stared at me for a long moment, then,

"Good Lord, no. Would I be so reckless?"

I stood up, walked over to him.

With a supreme effort, I didn't wallop him, said,

"You really don't want to fuck with Keefer. We have a witness who saw you bolt the door to the house where four people burned to death."

He was unfazed, asked,

"And will this witness testify?"

When I didn't reply, he pushed,

"Rather awkward case to actually prove, I would think. A judge would throw it out."

I said,

"You're making a basic assumption here that is wrong."

He was relishing this verbal chess, asked,

"Pray tell."

I said,

"You think it would be judged in court, we have a whole other method of dealing with a killer."

He mocked,

"Vigilante justice? How film noir of you."

I shook my head, turned to leave. James was standing behind me, asked,

"What's film noir?"

"As
   My
Body

Continues on its journey
My thoughts keep turning back

And
Bury
      Themselves
In days past."

(Gustave Flaubert, 1849)

As I tried to figure out what to do about Benjamin J., I considered the options.

1. Kill him.
2. Tell the Guards.
3. Do nothing.

Number 3 was what I excelled at.

Telling the Guards had proved futile. Killing him, phew-oh. I was spirit-spent on all the death that engulfed my life. Once, I had attempted to head for America, the great illusion, but it sustained me through many bad Februarys.

Ann Henderson, the shining love of my bedraggled life, was dead. She'd once asked me,

"What would your ideal life be like?"

Even I knew that if a woman asks you that, you better include her as part of the vision. Then and now, I didn't know, but I could flippantly reply,

"To drink ferociously and not have hangovers."

Like that would happen.

Ofttimes, I sat on Nemo's Pier, stared at the ocean for hours. I could yearn as an Olympic event.

I had recently read
Wild and Crazy Guys
By
Nick de Semlyen.

An account of the eighties' comedians Bill Murray, Eddie Murphy, John Belushi, Dan Aykroyd, Steve Martin. After *Ghostbusters*, Bill Murray was one of the hottest stars in the world. It didn't sit easy with him, to such an extent that he fucked off to France, studied philosophy at the Sorbonne.

That impressed the hell out of me.

One passage describing his daily life in Paris seemed as close to perfect as you'd get, especially if your mind was most ways fractured.

Before I lay out Bill Murray's Parisian day, here is a rundown on what was going on in Ireland, in its entire insane color.

Trump arrived in Ireland, having literally fist-bumped with the queen during his U.K. visit. He did have talks with Farage on the very last day that Theresa May was in office as prime minister.

Farage had 33 percent of the European vote and, if a general election were to be called, the Tories were looking like they'd be decimated. Brexit, in its third insane year, continued to avoid solution.

All over Europe the far right were on the rise.

In Ireland, Trump was a huge hit in the tiny village of Doonbeg, where his hotel was situated. His sons went to the local pub and got a fierce welcome, even the parish priest coming out to sing their praises.

Was this now what we were?

No wonder we embraced Katie Taylor's fifth world title.

We so desperately needed a hero.

I needed to savor a day in Bill Murray's Paris life to exorcise the sheer weirdness of what our country was experiencing.

Bill Murray had a routine. Every morning, wearing a battered pair of Converse tennis shoes, he strolled into Paris's 5th arrondissement, passing such landmarks as the majestic Val-de-Grâce church and the tropical Jardin de Plantes. Arriving at Sorbonne University, he climbed a steep spiral staircase.

At his destination, a hushed classroom, overlooking the Eiffel Tower, he sat at a desk for the day's lessons. When they were over, he headed back down, smoked a cigarette hand-rolled with Gitanes tobacco, bought lunch and popped into his favorite chocolatier for 150 grams of candy.

Then he treated himself to a silent movie at the Cinémathèque.

(Nick de Semlyn)

I could imagine such a day, a day that seemed surreally perfect. I replayed that passage so many times in my head that I could smell the Gitanes.

I'd probably have skipped the 150 grams of candy.

I called Keefer; had to. Benjamin J. had issued a direct threat so I had to warn him. He answered with

"Whatever you're selling, we got it."

I said,

"It's Jack."

He said,

"What's up?"

I told him, laid it out as it had gone down. He was silent for a beat, then,

"So what are you going to do?"

Good question, but I went with,

"What am *I* going to do?"

I did let a touch of granite leak over the question. He said,

"You're there, he's there, and it's not rocket science."

Fuck.

I tried,

"What does that mean?"

He sighed, said,

"Deal with it."

I changed tack, asked,

"How is Sara, our girl, doing?"

His voice changed. I could hear warmth. He said,

"She's a trouper, real gem, that kid. She and the falcon are a perfect storm."

I had to think about that, asked,

"Isn't that unusual? I mean, for a falcon that's used to another handler?"

He said,

"All I know is they are inseparable. She even sleeps in the barn with the bird."

The thought flashed through my mind.

Killers find each other.

Good Lord, where did that come from?

I knew I better ask for Keefer's new lady and, for the life of me, could I remember her name?

Could I fuck?

Something to do with music, yeah, definitely. Was it Melody? No, it had some Celtic connotation? I went with

"How is your, um, lady friend?"

Lame, huh?

At least I hadn't said "significant other." Keefer said,

"You've forgotten her name already."

I blustered,

"As if. I mean, seriously?"

He hung up.

* * *

Teddy Nuland. The name suggested someone jovial, with a playful temperament.

He was the county coroner, medical examiner. Nearing retirement, he was not jovial, but put him together with his single malt he became very chatty. Not fun company but certainly gripping.

I'd known him for years but it was only in the last few that he allowed me into his company, a small circle of friends he drank with. I'd given him a rare single malt that cost the kind of money that had you mutter,

"Fuck me."

In Forster Street there is a small pub named Ryan's that is so incongruous most people pass it by. It caters to select professionals. The atmosphere is subdued, a serious tone for serious drinking.

I dropped in there on a Tuesday evening, a time favored by Teddy. The barman, named Shane, looked a hundred. He kept chat to the minimum. The pub itself was like a drawing room from the fifties.

Teddy was already seated in his usual booth, reading the *Irish Times*, dressed in a fine suit that might have been fashionable in 1963. He was once a tall man but his profession had stooped him; thinning brown hair was styled in a very bad comb-over. His face seemed as if it were carved from the very stones of Connemara. The eyes, behind small glasses, were vibrant, hinting at a suppressed devilment and, indeed, he had a sharp cutting wit. Badly needed in his line of work.

I headed over, asked,

"Teddy, might I join you?"

He put the paper aside, took his glasses aside, said,

"Young Taylor."

I sat and Shane arrived with my pint and a short for Teddy. I didn't pay, you settled up when you left. Very civilized.

I asked,

"How have you been?"

He gave that serious thought, then,

"I expect to see you on my slab one of these days."

I said with absolute truth,

"God forbid."

You waited until Teddy hit his stride, meaning single malt number five, then his tongue threw caution to the wind. I asked,

"That book I gave you,

Herbert Lieberman's *City of the Dead*,

Did you read it?"

He nodded, said,

"Fairly accurate for a novel."

You could see his features alter slightly as he prepared to spill some trade secrets. He said,

"Strange case recently. You remember that fire some weeks back, the Americans and the miracle child?"

I said, casually,

"Terrible business."

He was quiet for a time and I thought he'd decided not to share, but then,

"Very odd. The fire was confined to the bottom part of the building, where the Americans died from smoke inhalation but, upstairs, the boy and a middle-aged woman."

He stopped, a look of horror on his face, and with all he'd seen, examined, he was years beyond shock. He said,

"The boy and the woman, I think she was the carer, their throats were cut."

I tried to process this, couldn't.

He ended with

"The devil of it is, they'd been killed at least twenty-four hours before the fire."

"An unappreciated miracle
Mutates
Into
An evil of such banality
That it almost
Passes
Unnoticed.
Almost."

(Fr. Edmund Dysart)

Keefer was to meet me in Garavan's. I'd rung him to say it was vital he come to town. He'd asked,

"Why don't you come out here, see Sara, tend to your falcon, meet Ceola."

Fuck.

I couldn't face the girl-child Sara yet. Needed to get some space since Teddy made his shock findings. Worse, if possible, he'd said the murder weapon was a serrated blade, like the one Sara carried at all times.

I made lame excuses but emphasized he had to meet me. He finally agreed, then,

"Got to tell you, this girl Sara, she's like the daughter I never had."

I was nursing my first pint when Keefer arrived. He was dressed less biker and more urban cowboy: new bandanna and crisp white shirt, dark jeans, boots that had a spit polish, and, I swear, a haircut.

I was about to order his pint and a shot when he said,

"Sparkling water is fine."

Not good. The news I had to lay on him did not warrant him sober, no way. I got a double Jay for myself and grabbed a table at the back. He gave me a long look, asked,

"What's so urgent?"

No way to sugarcoat it so I told it straight. He listened without comment. Finally, I ended with a description of the knife. I sat back, exhausted. He shook his head, said,

"You're unbelievable."

All I had was,

"What?"

He said with total coldness,

"Some drunk quack spins you a wild yarn about time of death and murder weapon and *you*, the fucking ace investigator, the top *private eye*, deduce it's a young girl who has suffered abuse of every description."

Then he stood up, threw some money on the table, said,

"I used to wonder why all your friends left you. They got killed or just fucked off. But now I get it. You're a paranoid prick with no loyalty, no real empathy, just a sodden drunk who thinks the odd book he scans gives him gravitas. I'd pity you if you weren't doing such a fine job of that yer own self but, get this asshole, stay the hell away from me and my family."

He strode out.

What could I say?

Thank you for sharing?

I was in Crowe's, nursing my battered ego and a boilermaker on a Monday evening. Quiz night.

A guy was shouting into his phone beside me.

Like this,

"Sell, sell now, the shares will drop by morning."

Yeah, I then realized his phone was dead. He was shouting into empty space, like most of us in one way or another.

iPhones, the modern plague.

iPhones are a blessing or a curse, depending on which neighborhood of the debate you choose. But one thing they have killed is the pub quiz. Unless you ban the phones for the evening, as Crowe's did for their Monday event. Two teams, captained by Bohermore lads, Tommy McGrath and John Casserly. I'd forgotten the quiz as I went there for a quiet time to ponder the whole Sara/Keefer situation.

I was sitting in the back as the quiz teams piled in. I couldn't really leave as they'd be more than a little offended. I tried to keep my head down as the questions began, heard,

"Who captained the Galway hurling team in 2005?"

Fucked if I knew.

"Who was in *Downton Abbey* and *Game of Thrones*?"

Tommy shouted at me.

"Jack, you should know this."

I said,

"Iain Glen."

John's team objected to me being consulted. I was merely a spectator.

The questions continued,

"Who was on the Irish pound note?"

"Who wrote *Sex and Death at Merlin Park Hospital*?"

I knew this but said nothing.

In exasperation, John asked,

"Jack?"

I said,

"Kevin Higgins."

I was beginning to feel just a tad informed until

"Name three Irish presidents."

I finished my drink, took my ignorant leave.

Homelessness was a major problem. Hundreds of families living in direct provision schemes. The number of patients on trolleys in the hospitals was shocking. Boris Johnson was leader of the Tories now and getting out of bed (or off a trolley) was daunting.

I'd been walking down Water Lane, then turned into the field that leads to Hidden Valley. A man emerged from the trees, a tent pitched behind him. He was shoeless and looked traumatized. I took some notes from my pocket, offered them, he said,

"No, I'm good, but thank you."

Manners were so rare these days that for a moment I was speechless, then I foisted the notes on him, suggested,

"You'd be better off pitching the tent up the top, would protect you from the late-night gobshites."

He allowed himself the tiniest of smiles. Then he asked me a question that would haunt me for a long time. He asked,

"Are there rats?"

I couldn't answer that for a myriad of reasons so went with

"Get yourself a small terrier. Not only will he deal with any rodents, he'd be great company."

He considered that, then stuck out his hand,

"Thanks man, you've been a great help."

I took his hand, shook it with a feeling of utter forlornness.

I checked on him a few days later. His tent was there but torn to shreds, his meager belongings scattered to the ruthless wind. Of him, there was sign.

Ireland in the year of Our Lord 2019.

The Epiphany of Benjamin J. Cullen

Benjamin J. had never really been taken by surprise.
Few events shocked him, and he was the bringer of
shock.

The morning of Tuesday the eighteenth, he found
the kitchen in a mess. James Powell was not the tidi-
est of guests/employees.

Benjamin read him the riot act, culminating with,
My house, my rules.

As Benjamin finished shaving, he was debating,
"Scrambled or fried eggs for breakfast?"

James came behind him, pulled his head back, cut
his throat with one deep lethal slash.

Then he dragged Benjamin by the scruff of his
clean-shaven neck, out through the spacious hall,
trailing a line of blood, opened the front door, flung
the body out across the drive, shouted,

"*Not your house!*"

James was eating scrambled eggs when the Guards
came bursting through the front door.

When asked why he'd murdered Benjamin,
He asked, in total bewilderment,
"Who?"

James Cromwell is one of those character actors that people recognize but never know his name. They go,

"Don't tell me, I know."

But they don't.

His one leading role was with a pig, literally, in *Babe*.

He gave numerous heavyweight performances in movies such as *The General's Daughter* and *L.A. Confidential*.

I mention him as on a sunny Friday morning I was availing myself of a brief shot of sunshine on Eyre Square when James Cromwell came striding toward me.

No, of course, it wasn't him but the spitting image. Tall, *rangy* as they say in the States. A weather-walloped face, distinctive nose, in the age range of good seventies or not so fine sixties. Dressed in a dark suit with, oddly enough, sparkling trainers, dressed as the song goes, like,

"A walking contradiction."

He stood over me, said,

"Jack Taylor."

I nodded and he asked,

"Might I have a word?"

I said,

"Seems you're having it."

He smiled briefly, then,

"I'm Edmund Dysart."

His accent, ting of U.S. but more like English was a second language. I studied him for a moment, ventured,

"You're a priest."

Staggered him but he recovered, asked,

"Why would you think that?"

The devil was in me to say *I can smell you*.

But a bit harsh so I said,

"My life is beset by the clergy."

He thought about that, said,

"I'm no longer a priest."

Right.

I said,

"Once a priest . . ."

He asked,

"May I buy you a drink?"

I agreed and said,

"You're definitely not a priest anymore."

If he found that insulting, he let it slide. We went to Richardson's at the top of the square, got a table. I ordered pints and he didn't demur but, unpriest-like, he paid for the round.

We skimmed the heads of the pints, then he began,

"I was sent to Guatemala for various sins of my past,"

Paused, added quickly,

"Nothing to do with children, I swear."

Then he continued.

"The caravan trail of people heading for the U.S. border had just begun, a long line of destitute folk walking or hoping to walk through so many countries. It was in Guatemala that I first heard of a *miracle child*, a girl surrounded by light, but it was soon discredited, then other stories began of this girl/woman attaching herself to young boys, declaring them her brother, and evoking sympathy."

He sighed with tremendous weariness, then,

"More stories of young boys found with their throats cut, and rumors turned to *La Niña del Diablo*."

He looked at me, asked,

"Do I need to translate?"

I ventured,

"Devil child."

He signaled to the barman, another pint and shorts of scotch.

I hadn't the heart to correct him. Scotch! And figured he was paying so . . .

He took a gulp of his, then,

"I met her once, but once was more than enough."

I tried the scotch. It would suffice.

His eyes had a far sheen to them when he continued.

"She seemed the essence of innocence at first, with a charisma that invited you closer, and then I noticed a small boy almost hiding behind her. I asked,

"*Este es su hermano?*" (Your brother?)

He now looked right at me, said,

"She was peeling an apple, slowly, deliberately, with a knife that glinted off her eyes. She said, with a kind of a hiss . . ."

He took a moment, then,

"She said, *Fuck off, priest.*"

His whole body went into a minor spasm but he reined it in, said,

"Then she turned to the boy, offered him a slice of the apple, cajoled, *Eat, my sweet.*"

He sighed, continued.

"I threw my rosary beads at her. I still am not sure why but it hit her neck and it *sizzled,* left the mark of the crucifix just below her jawline."

He shuddered violently, said,

"She said, 'My mother cursed you at Camargue, I curse you anew.'"

He said,

"I had indeed crossed paths with a psycho woman in France and this child, this spawn of evil, was her daughter. There is a legend there of a child, Sara: The Gypsies worship her. I had gone to see this creature who was supposed to be possessed. She had a cobra tattooed on her arm. She cursed me, told me her daughter would be the cause of my death, that she would find me in Guatemala. Now this was long before I was banished to that country by the Church."

I felt something cold, sinister creep along my spine, needed a moment to regroup, and asked,

"Why are you here?"

He said.

"Because she is here."

In near contempt, I said,

"You seriously think a fourteen-year-old girl is capable of such . . ."

I searched for a word, got

"Malevolence?"

He looked at me in what seemed to be disbelief, said,

"In your own country, have you not recently tried two thirteen-year-old boys for a horrific murder?"

He was referring to the Ana Kriegel case, our very own version of the Jamie Bulger case in the U.K. Two teenage boys had lured a fourteen-year-old girl to a derelict building, tortured, raped, and murdered her.

The details of the boys' preparations to kill were so terrible that even the media practiced restraint in their reporting.

What was known was that Boy A, as he was called for legal reasons, had over a thousand videos of porn that involved animals, murder, satanic rites, mutilation, which he brought to the murder site with tape, knife, homemade zombie mask. The girl had more than a hundred wounds on her body but she had fought like a tigress so that Boy A had a host of injuries.

Ana, adopted from Siberia when she was two, had been a beautiful girl but shy, vulnerable, sensitive, badly bullied at school for her stature and otherness. She longed for friendship.

Both boys were found guilty, the youngest convicted killers ever in the history of the state.

I asked Dygart,

"When you find her, what then?"

Without hesitation, he said,

"I'm going to kill her."

"The
    Annals
    of
    Human wisdom
Fall
  Silent
    When faced
      With the feral
      Within
      Us."

(William Girondi)

June 23, 2019.

As I contemplated how to prevent an ex-priest from killing a supposed child, the world was thus:

Jimmy Kimmel on Trump's launch of his presidential campaign in Florida:

"The stadium had a capacity of 20,000

Or, as Trump calls it,

A million."

Sara Collins (comedian) on the Remainer frustration that Labour leader Corbyn won't take a stand against Brexit:

"Couldn't we just tell Corbyn that Israel is behind Brexit?"

Trump ready to launch rockets on Iran:

"We were cocked and loaded."

Raisa Carolan, a child survivor of the Chernobyl disaster who was adopted and now lives in Ireland, on the wave of tourism to Chernobyl following the hit TV show about the disaster:

"It's disgraceful to all the people who died and sacrificed them-selves so others could live, people need to think before they decide to take selfies."

Owen McDonagh was a young Guard. I'd met him years before, when he worked as a cashier for Dunne's. We'd become friendly discussing TV shows. I'd lent him *Preacher*, season one, and cemented a friendship. One day, as he was overwhelmed with customers being especially demanding, I'd asked,

"Ever think of another line of work?"

He asked,

"Any suggestions?"

I'd said without much consideration,

"You could do worse than join the Guards."

He did.

I'd meant it as a casual off-the-cuff remark but he'd gone and joined. He'd recently been assigned to Galway and we met up from time to time. He loved being a Guard, reminded me of the long-ago time I'd had such aspirations. He tipped me off to various cases where my name was mentioned. Never in a good light, alas.

A Thursday, his day off, he'd phoned me, asked if we could meet. He had to be careful as a friendship with me was not a route to advancement in the force.

We met in the Crane Bar, not a place much favored by the cops. He'd been to the gym, was dressed in sweats, looking fit and fresh, not anything that could ever be remotely applied to my own self.

He was drinking pints of water after a vigorous workout; I was on pints as always. We did the usual catch-up but he had something on his mind, so I pushed.

"What's up, Owen?"

He dithered for a while, then,

"The suspected arsonist Benjamin J. Cullen was found murdered."

I immediately thought,

Keefer.

I asked,

"How? How was he killed?"

He said,

"His throat was cut."

My mind roared.

Definitely Keefer. Or, God forbid, Sara? Or, heaven forbid, the both of them.

But Owen's next words canceled that. He said,

"A mental patient staying with Cullen did the deed."

I never expected that.

Nor, it seems, did Benjamin J.

Owen continued,

"I was one of the first responders, as Mr. Cullen had been thrown out his front door after his throat was cut. We found the accused sitting having scrambled eggs and . . ."

He had to pause to compose himself, then,

"He was using the knife to eat his eggs."

Now Owen looked like he might throw up, said,

"I'll never use ketchup again, at least not on eggs."

I finally could put it off no longer; I had to see Keefer. He'd left the pickup truck at the rear of my apartment so I climbed in that, with a heavy heart, and at first I was nearly relieved when it didn't start.

Thank fuck, I thought.

Tried again and the engine turned over, much in time to the heavy beat of my heart. I pulled into traffic and headed for the country.

My time on the farm with Keefer and the falcon had been one of the most peaceful episodes of my life in between the interludes of violence. I didn't dwell on Jericho, who'd come to the farm to kill me. She never left the farm.

I listened to the radio. Jimmy Norman, now running Norman Media, was explaining his use of drones as a vital part of his media company. It was reassuring to hear of drones that were not part of U.S. foreign policy.

I got to the farm by noon, pulled up beside the small cottage to the back that had been my home, if briefly. I'd brought supplies.

Booze.

Steaks.

Chocolate. (For Sara? Maybe.)

And a pile of books from Charlie Byrne's bookshop.

I wasn't entirely sure if they were peace offerings/bribes/distraction or a blend of all three. A young woman came out of the main building. In her late twenties, I guessed, with long dark hair, sallow complexion, a serious expression, wearing faded jeans and a well-washed Rolling Stones T-shirt.

I got out of the truck, hazarded,

"Ceola?"

She smiled, a gorgeous one, and up close she smelled of patchouli and a sweet nature. She had a Romany vibe, more Gypsy than civilian. She said,

"Jack Taylor."

And then she hugged me.

I don't do hugs.

May be my generation, we didn't come from the kind of families that expressed affection. The most you could hope for was,

"Don't bring the Guards to our door!"

This hug was more desperate than affectionate. She whispered,

"Thank God you're here."

Keefer appeared, shouted,

"Hands off my chick, Taylor!"

Chick, like, fuck sakes.

He didn't hug me.

He asked,

"So what brings you here?"

I reached into the truck, dragged out the box of supplies, said,

"Thought you might need re-up."

He took the box, asked,

"Any bourbon in there?"

I said,

"Kentucky's finest and some serious chocolate for the girls."

He handed the box to Ceola, said,

"Put these away, lass, but break out the bourbon to welcome our guest."

I didn't see any sign of Sara. I asked,

"Where is our miracle girl?"

He gave me a look that was more warning than warmth, said,

"She's out with the falcon, every hour of the day with that bird."

I asked,

"Might we have a word in private?"

He gestured around the farm, said,

"Doesn't get more private, pilgrim."

I began,

"Benjamin J. Cullen was murdered, his throat cut."

He took that in, then near exploded.

"You think I did it?"

Paused to catch his breath, then, in a tone of dripping sarcasm, continued,

"Or maybe the girl? Fuck sakes, she traveled to Galway, did the deed, then got herself back here, you dumb cracker, that what you think happened?"

I had to rein in my anger, then tried,

"I wasn't finished. I was going to tell you they already have the man who did it."

The air of violence was heavy around us. Few fights as bitter as friends who fall out. I breathed heavily and he sneered,

"Weren't you hoping to tell me of the ex-priest who came to Ireland to find Sara, or was that to be the *big* reveal?"

That was the sad truth of it. I said nothing, so he said,

"That pious piece of shit was here, told me his insane theory about Sara. I put the shotgun in his face and pulled the trigger."

I literally rocked back.

He let me reel like that until he said,

"I told him next time the shotgun will be loaded."

Keefer looked over my shoulder. I turned to see Sara, the falcon perched on her arm. The sun behind them gave the appearance of a statue, carved in ice; both were motionless. It was hard to say where the bird ended, so close they seemed, like one lethal force. I noticed the scar in the shape of a crucifix below her jawline. It seemed to throb like a resentment.

Keefer smiled, said with a forced cheer,

"Sweetheart, look who's come to visit you."

A few tense moments, then she handed off the falcon to Keefer, who said,

"I'll give you guys a moment."

She stared at me for a time then moved toward me, arms outstretched. She was no longer the vulnerable child, if ever she had been, but was now a young woman, looking way more than the supposed fourteen, an air of supreme confidence about her.

She was fingering her neck and I realized she was in fact rubbing my daughter's gold miraculous medal, then her arms went round me.

She leaned in real close, whispered,

"Fuck off, cunt."

"The Miracle of Small Proportion."

Known colloquially as the *small miracle*
Occurs when a person provides
A major service/assistance
To a person they despise.
It is as rare as it is small.

(Comte De Brun, 1900–34)

I'd returned from Keefer's by cab. Keefer had said,

"You no longer have use of my truck and don't come here again."

As I got into the cab, I turned to see Sara standing by the house, a smile of utter malevolence creeping across her pretty face.

I knew the cabdriver, Hugh McEntee. His mother (McEntee-Kennedy), Ena, had saved many girls from the infamous Magdalene. He let his eyes sweep across the farm, said,

"Worth a few bob."

I grunted some vague assent.

The radio was tuned to Keith Finnegan. He was paying tribute to Kitty Kelly, who'd died at the age of 105, and Hugh asked me,

"Did you know her?"

Everybody knew Kitty. She'd worked Births, Marriages Department in the county buildings. She knew your date of birth the minute you walked into the office. Not too many of that caliber anymore.

She was always cheerful and if you met her on the street she'd greet you with total warmth, like this,

"Young Taylor, you look mighty."

I'd met her on the day of her ninetieth birthday and she told me she was going to have a ninety-nine for the occasion—that is, the ice cream cone with a flake on top.

Hugh said,

"Kitty attributed her longevity to a glass of sherry every night, even in the nursing home. The nurses made sure she had that."

I tried to balance that lovely story against the sheer evil of whatever the girl-child Sara was.

It only helped a little, like a rosary against the storm.

I spent a whole day in a blue funk, one of those awful "sit in a chair, stare at the wall, feel unable to rise to anything" ones, the mind in a blitzkrieg of guilt, rage, frustration, and every voice in your head screaming,

"You are a worthless piece of shit!"

A strangely level voice asking,

"Seriously, name one good thing you can be proud of."

As a gauge of how low I was, I didn't smoke, drink, or take a Xanax.

Did I wallow in that hell?

Yes.

Wouldn't it be wonderful if, after you stood up, full of new resolve, full of a hard-won belief, that you were now a whole fresh page?

Like fuck.

When I did eventually stir, I made some coffee, as bitter as a translated prayer. I showered, the water scalding, the water lashing me. I'd often wondered what exactly the term *self-flagellation* truly meant.

I wondered no more.

I dressed in a faded T-shirt advertising the Rory Gallagher tour, so you can guess just how old it was. Clean 501s and, it being summer, worn moccasins that loved my feet.

Took a long neglected book from the shelf, from K. C. Constantine's the Mario Balzic series. Most people never heard of him, and the fact that he remained totally anonymous wasn't going to raise his profile.

I was half-engaged in the book when the doorbell rang. Did I welcome the distraction?

No.

Opened it to Father Malachy.

He looked terrible, like ill. He was dressed like a civilian, a tired unironed shirt and gray leggings with the cuff that no one on the planet can wear with panache.

He had a blackthorn stick, like a prop from *The Quiet Man*, and he was leaning heavily on it. He barked,

"Don't leave me standing here like a bollix."

I waved my arm in a sarcastic sweep of welcome, because welcome he surely wasn't. He limped in, sank into a chair with lots of sighing, puffing, generally milking the whole invalid vibe. He said,

"Don't stand there like an ejit, get a person a drink."

I was very impressed with my own restraint but it had its limit. I poured him a Jay, asked with bitterness,

"Ice?"

He near snapped the glass, peered at the level, asked,

"You rationing it?"

I looked at the watch I didn't have on my wrist, said,

"Tops, you have one minute to get your mouth in gear, else I'll kick your arse so fast out the door you won't know what happened."

He looked hurt, I mean as if I had *offended him*, then,

"There's no need for that, Jack."

Use of my first name, sure sign some heavy shite was winging its way. He said/whined,

"No need for that at all."

I poured a coffee, wanted to lash some Jay, but one of us, I felt, better try for control. I asked,

"Why are you here?"

He said,

"I need you to kill me."

Over the years, I have sworn a hundred, a thousand times that I'd like to kill Malachy. Few have tested me as he has. But now he was asking me?

I went,

"What?"

His head down, he said,

"I have motor neuron disease, in the advanced stages. From the time of diagnosis, it kills within three years unless you are Stephen Hawking. I am already losing control over my hands, feet, legs, and arms. I won't be able to talk, walk, or swallow, then I won't be able to breath without some machine hooked up to me, then I'll die."

I said,

"Fuck me."

Malachy was not one of life's smilers. Grimace, yes, often, but smiles, no. He smiled now, said,

"No, fuck me."

I got the bottle of Jay, poured for us both. He said,

"Good health."

He took a drink, said,

"I can't live without being able to do anything so they'll ship me off to one of those clerical hospitals where they hide the worst priests and I'll die being abused by angry, frustrated nuns."

I asked,

"They have such places?"

He laughed, asked,

"They're the Church, what do you think?"

I thought they did.

He put his glass down, the tremor in his hand causing the glass to do a mini jig on the surface. He asked,

"So will you, Jack, will you help me die?"

Phew-oh.

Wrong on so many levels.

I asked,

"Isn't suicide like the worst thing on your guys' agenda? Eternal damnation, no burial in consecrated ground, burn in hell, and all the attendant fury?"

He smiled, well pleased, said,

"See, here's the beauty of it, you'll be killing me, so it's not suicide."

Aw, for fuck sakes. I said,

"For fuck sakes, that won't fly."

He wasn't fazed, said,

"If you put phenobarbital in a nice glass of champagne, it will be like I'm going to sleep and you won't have told me when exactly you're going to do it."

I wanted to shake him but he had a fine old tremor already in play. I said,

"So let me see if I follow this. Every time I see you, I give you a lethal glass of champers, a kind of clerical Russian roulette."

He actually *tut-tutted*, prepared to bear with my density, said,

"But I have selected the day, my birthday, which is around the corner."

Of all the insane thoughts storming my brain, I asked,

"Champagne? You don't drink that shite."

He sighed, patience ebbing, said,

"But it will be my birthday."

Was there logic there?

Fuck if I could find it.

Then my mind cleared a bit, asked,

"What about me, murder and all that mortal shit stuff?"

He waved that away with

"You have so many sins, will God notice?"

It was all so weird, unbelievable. I snarled,

"Where the fuck do you think I'm going to get phenobarbital if, and big *if*, I even for one mad moment considered doing the deed?"

His patience really was wearing as thin as a nun in Lent. He said,

"You're in the life."

Whoa!

Hold the fucking phone. I snapped.

"*In the life*? What, you've been binge-watching *The Sopranos*?"

He reached in his pocket, took out a vape, said,

"Won't be needing this shite no more."

And with what I must admit was a near perfect throw landed it in the wastebasket, then took out the ultimate coffin nails, Major, the green pack that are so strong you need two people to inhale.

He managed to get the cig in his mouth but trying to flick a Bic lighter was too much for the shake in his fingers. Exasperated I grabbed it from him, fired him up. Did he thank me? Did he fuck. He said,

"Give me back my Bic."

Enveloped in smoke, he said,

"Don't be modest, Jack boy, you have dope dealers coming out of yer arse."

Lovely PC turn of phrase.

I asked,

"How do you know about phenobarbital?"

A sly smile, then,

"I've been watching *Mary Kills People*; even better than Google for DIY offing yer own self."

Offing yer self.

His vocabulary really had changed, if not improved. He stood up, crushed the cig beneath his foot, on my floor! Said,

"I have to go. I'm glad you agreed to be my executioner."

God almighty.

I said,

"You ever say anything even in the neighborhood of that, you can get your own rope."

He gave a short merry laugh, said,

"Jaysus, you need to lighten up. No wonder you look so old. Here's something to cheer you up."

I could hardly wait. He said,

"A young lad is being forced to drink liters of cider by some older boys: What is the term for that?"

I said,

"Business as usual?"

Impish grin, then he said,

"Cider bullying."

He gave me a playful punch in the shoulder, laughed again, said,

"Ah, Jack, you'll be the death of me."

* * *

T. S. Eliot wrote about the dread of

The mental emptiness . . .
Leaving only the growing terror of nothing to think about.

This was not my dilemma.
I had two very focused events to weigh.
Kill a child (Sara).
Kill a priest (Malachy).
God in heaven.
I sat looking out my bay window, seeing/not seeing the ocean stretching to the Aran Islands. Asked aloud,
"How in holy hell did I get to such a fierce dilemma in my life?"
I had a black coffee in front of me, with a glass of Jay riding point. My mind was a sewer of horror. I could do nothing but, like, that was going to solve anything.
I remembered some lines of Rilke.

Still though, alas
I invoke you, almost deadly birds of the soul.

A knock at the door. I welcomed any respite from my own torrid company, hoped it might be Malachy with a change of mind. He was a priest. Wouldn't all his clerical training, his indoctrination force him to pull back from the abyss?

But then, Malachy was no ordinary priest; far from it.

Opened the door to Dysart, the ex-priest, the one who wanted to kill Sara, who had gone to Keefer's place and had a shotgun shoved in his face.

I said,

"Come in. I'm nearly glad to see you."

"God sends your ex
Into your life again
To see if you've learned anything
Or
If
You're still the same dumb fuck."

(Keefer)

Before I could front Dysart on his poor showing in front of Keefer, he took me totally by surprise with

"Tell me, Jack, what has scared you in your life. I mean the stuff that haunts you for days after with its image."

I was fairly spoiled for choice there. I went for evasion.

"Well, the two movies by Ari Aster, *Hereditary* and *Midsommar*."

When I was a Garda cadet I saw Polanski's *Repulsion*, which lingered for months in my head.

But for the sheer moment of terror, when my hair stood on end, that would be when the bag moved with a body in it in *Audition*.

He was annoyed, said,

"You're being flippant. I mean, have you ever been face-to-face with utter evil?"

Was he fucking kidding? I snarled,

"Don't be a supercilious prick. I've been right up and personal with evil on a nearly fucking weekly basis."

His hand went up; he let out a fake,

"*Whoa*, dial it down a notch, buddy."

After Malachy, after the fracas with Keefer, I went into meltdown, grabbed him by the throat, spat,

"You don't come into my home and tell me to *dial it fucking down*."

287

He was scared. I thought for a minute the white cold fury wouldn't ebb and I'd kill him, but some *epiphany* hit me from left side and I let him go.

Much later, when all this was done, I'd be able to put words to the epiphany but not then, not there. I was too wrought up.

I slumped back, as if I'd been the one struck, and thought I might keel over.

Dysart was shaking, trying to catch his breath. He looked at me, said,

"A moment there, you had true evil in your soul."

I whispered,

"Believe it."

"An
Epiphany
Is
an
Experience
of
Sudden
and
Striking
Realization"

(dictionary definition)

I gave Dysart a large Jay and he produced a crumpled pack of Camels, lit one bruised cig with a heavy Zippo, said,

"I was off these for ten years, then I came to Ireland."

I said,

"Go ahead, blame us. You must have British blood."

He rubbed his neck, muttered,

"I thought you were going to kill me."

I looked at him, said,

"I was."

That put a kink in chat for a while, then he said,

"I met your wife, sorry, ex-wife, at meetings."

The fuck he said?

I went,

"What?"

Drinking the Jameson, he, brazen as a wild pup, tells me,

"AA meetings. Kiki has a year now."

I wanted to strangle him again, asked,

"But you're drinking and aren't those meetings supposed to help? And, mainly, aren't those meetings meant to be anonymous. Isn't that the fucking point?"

He said,

"I can control my drinking. It's okay once you know when to cut back."

I used all my wisdom, all my experience, all my failed methods of a way to drink without being slaughtered, summed it up for him with

"Horseshite."

Kiki.

Phew-oh, to capture Kiki in a brief summary.

Years back, after I'd investigated the suicide of young girls, I fled to London and I mean I was truly *fleeing*.

Spent a year on Ladbroke Grove, wasted, like the character in Patrick Hamilton's *Hangover Square*. Thank God, most of it is a blur, my very own version of *London fog*.

Got married, yeah, fuck me.

To a German metaphysician, Kiki,

The top had barely settled on our Guinness when we got divorced and I slunk back to Galway with a leather coat I bought on Camden Lock. The lyrics of Van Morrison's "Madame George" wafting in my head.

Such are the vagaries of my life that in my holdall were albums by Rory Gallagher and the Pogues. I was barely a week back home when the leather coat was stolen, much like my marriage.

Years later, Kiki turned up with a gorgeous little girl. She said,

"This is your daughter."

Like holy fuck.

Right?

Took a time but I bonded with the little girl and my heart was fit to burst. I could hardly breathe for sheer joy.

The child was murdered right in front of me.

And Job wailed he got a rough ride?

Kiki in her own form of insane grief took up with a psycho known as *Silence*. A savage ice-cold calculating predator that became fixated with destroying slowly everything and everyone I held dear.

I was slow to react as I was in a state of traumatic paralysis until, finally, I stole a high-powered rifle and gut shot the fucker in the drive of the home he shared with Kiki.

Kiki went back to the booze with fixed fatalism.

Our child was buried in Rahoon Cemetery, made famous by James Joyce with his ode to Nora Barnacle's dead lover. With apologies to Joyce, I saw it as

The place where my dead daughter lies.

There is no greater grief. None.

Dysart held out his glass and I snapped,

"How can you attend AA meetings when you drink and it seems you drink like a sailor?"

He gave a self-satisfied smile that riled me. I pushed further.

"You went half-cocked or, now I imagine, half in the bag, to see Keefer, got a shotgun in your mouth?"

He said,

"I wanted to get the perimeters, not to mention the parameters, for when we go to take the girl."

The sheer bloody cheek of the prick. I said,

"I'll take care of the girl."

He lit up, amazed, echoed,

"You will?"

"On one condition."

He agreed foolishly fast, said,

"Name it?"

I said,

"Phenobarbital."

Now I had his full attention. He asked,

"What on earth are you planning? You're not going to kill yourself just when we are bonding?"

He really did need a wallop to the side of the head. I lied,

"I'm going to go to the farm, reconcile with Keefer, bring a celebratory bottle of bourbon. The devil child likes a wee dram. She'll get a real kick out of her dose."

He gave a smile that lurked somewhere between the sacred and profane, very unpleasant. He asked,

"But won't you kill your buddy, your *bro*"—he leaned heavily on the sarcasm—"too?"

I gave him a nasty smile right back and, when I put my mind to it, I can go dark with the worst of them. I said,

"He regards Sara as if she were his own. When he sees her go, he'll murder me and come looking for you also, I imagine."

He rubbed his hands in glee, said,

"You're quite the evil little fooker, aren't you?"

I said,

"I was taught by Jesuits and one important note."

He was reveling in this, the bad bastard, asked,

"Pray tell."

I said,

"You ever refer to Keefer as my *bro* again I'll kick the living shite out of you."

He laughed, said,

"Scary. Anyway, back to the issue. I can get Seconal, crush up ten, you'd kill them both and maybe all the animals on the farm."

I asked,

"Where is the Church currently on suicide and priests?"

He was wary, tried,

"We, or rather they, regard it as a mortal sin."

I was no wiser, pushed,

"But do priests their own selves kill themselves?"

He was now very antsy, said,

"Well, I'm no expert but drink is a form of slow suicide."

Before I could ask more, he said,

"Kiki wants to meet you."

Lord wept. I snarled,

"What? You're a dating bureau?"

He gave me a patient look, said,

"The poor woman is lonely."

I stood up, said very quietly,
"Time for you to fuck off out of here."
He put his arms out, asked,
"Hug?"
I could only think he was on serious medication.

The Hummingbird

At the exact moment of death
You lose twenty-one grams
Which is believed
To be the weight of your soul.
It is also the exact weight of a hummingbird.

The Galway Arts Festival was in full show; Burt Bacharach was headlining.

On a Sunday night. Now, I don't know how God feels about ol' Burt but here's the thing. The three weeks preceding the festival we had scorching heat, a rarity of biblical proportion for the city and, worse, humidity.

The Sunday night after this heat wave, the heavens opened, thunder, lashing rain that made you reach for holy water.

I went to the exhibition that people told me was

Unmissable.

Beautiful.

Awesome.

Sam Jinks on his second visit to Galway with sculptures made from human hair, wax that eerily seemed like skin, and shown in a black space lit only by the exhibits.

I know how fucking contrary I am but the exhibits freaked the shite out of me. I've seen too many bodies in morgues to actually go see it in a festival.

I know, I know, art is to provoke, so it sure as hell did that.

But being some kind of masochist, I wasn't done. Oh no. I went to a play based on Rosemary Kennedy, her years of confinement in a madhouse, with a soundtrack of discordant music shredding my nerves.

I swore to readdict myself to Xanax.

* * *

"There is no refuge from confession

   But suicide, and

   Suicide is confession."

Daniel Webster.

Bizarre as it sounds, this was printed on a T-shirt worn by Malachy as we met to discuss the details of his murder/suicide.

I said,

"What the fuck, are you advertising your imminent death?"

He was offended, said,

"I bought you a T-shirt too, do you want to see it?"

Fuck.

I said,

"Go on then."

Just a tiny bit curious, God only knows what this was.

He handed me a black T, XL, with gold writing; it read

        Dead is

        Not always

        The worst thing

Stephen King.

I was lost for words, none of them containing any hint of thanks, said,

"I'm lost for words."

He was delighted, urged,

"Put it on."

I figured he'd lost any vague semblance of sanity, tenuous as it was in the best of clerical years. I asked,

"You mean, like now?"

He did.

I didn't put it on then or ever.

But was he finished. Was he fuck?

He reached into his priest suit (ash-sprinkled collar—at least I'd prefer to think ash rather than dandruff), took out a flashy decorated box and, I kid you not, with a freaking bow, said,

"'Tis to mark our bond."

I admit to once seeing an episode of *Friends*, where Joey is wearing a godawful chunky bracelet and gives Chandler an identical one, saying cheerfully,

"We're bracelet buddies."

And Chandler ruefully concedes in horror with,

"And that's what they'll call us."

I said,

"Can I open it later?"

Bitter disappointment flooded his face, so I said,

"I'll open it."

Did, to find a heavy hummingbird on a silver chain. He said,

"That bird marks the moment between life and the transition to eternal life."

I said,

"Wow."

Thinking,

Won't eternal life for a suicide, especially a priest suicide, mean eternal roasting in hellfire?

I said,

"You're full of surprises."

He put a hand to my shoulder, said,

"This week is my birthday."

The Ellison Epiphany (No. 5)

I was in my apartment reading *The Weight* by Andrew Vachss, an author who never ceases to amaze me. He is a

Stone warrior.

A granite poet.

Champion of the marginalized.

Never-ending pursuer of pedophiles.

He was that rare event, a writer I admired as much for his art as for his crusades for justice.

A gentle knock on my door. I almost didn't hear it. Anyone comes to my door, they come banging and walloping. I opened the door to a waif, a pixie, a dote in miniature.

Ceola.

Keefer's girlfriend. I had met her only once, when she hugged me at the farm and whispered she was so glad I was there. I'd felt then that something was seriously amiss but Keefer had run me off.

Now here she was.

Her face was tired, distressed. She was dressed in mid-Goth/grunge style: short battered black leather jacket, jeans with more holes than WikiLeaks, Doc Marten worn-to-bits boots, a T-shirt with a faded Brian Jones picture and the logo/question:

"Who murder-dah Brian?"

I thought it was simply a misspelling but learned later, after Ceola's death, that it was patois.

I urged,

"Come in."

She did.

She looked around, and I saw it briefly as she might, a basically bare space with a bookcase, books of course, my Garda coat on the one hook, large TV, boxed sets close by. She said,

"Pretty Zen."

I said,

"Pretty poor, is what."

She smiled, though her heart wasn't much in there. I offered,

"Drink?"

She lit up, near gasped,

"Gosh, yes."

Sounded like,

Golly gosh!

Her accent was mid-Atlantic with a tiny hint of newly acquired Irish lilt. I got us healthy drinks—in that I mean large pour, no ice. She took a fine dollop of hers, asked,

"Mind if I roll up?"

She meant actual tobacco and rolled a cig with fast practiced moves, then lit up with practiced ease. I waited until she was ready, then she said,

"Thank you for letting me in, for the drink, for . . ."

Paused.

"For not being a bollix."

I smiled, asked,

"What's on your mind?"

She finished the drink and cig, seemed to chill, then said,

"My real name is Ellison Riley. My mother is Romanian, my dad is Scottish."

She continued,

"I was almost a professional violinist but dope got in the way."

Then she smiled, added,

"Dopes too."

I liked her sense of humor. She'd fucking need it.

I poured her another Jay and she knocked that back too. I didn't advise caution. I mean, seriously, me? I asked again,

"What's up?"

Sounding like a lame ejit, but I felt we were drifting off point.

She went very quiet then.

"Keefer has become besotted by Sara. He is convinced she is the daughter he never had and the sly bitch plays him like, if you'll excuse the awful pun, a fiddle. She hates me, and I know because she told me so, said she would get rid of me ASAP. I can't tell Keefer as he already thinks I'm jealous of her, which maybe I am. I had a Siamese cat named Concerto—do forgive all the musical references. Concerto was a gift from my old music tutor. I loved her like a baby."

She stopped, then regrouped, said,

"You can guess the next bit."

Alas, I could, said with a heavy heart,

"She killed the cat."

A sob escaped her. She said,

"That knife with the serrated blade, she gutted her, then last night I woke to find her holding that blade to my throat. She whispered to me in Romanian. She is fluent in many tongues, none of them civil. She said,

"Leave tomorrow, cunt."

Phew-oh.

I asked,

"What are you going to do now?"

She sighed deeply, said,

"I'm going to take a few days to pull myself together, then I'll go back there, face the bitch down. I can't leave Keefer with her. Eventually she'll take him out. It seems to be her gig."

I said,

"You could run."

Sounded good to me.

No.

She wouldn't do that, said,

"Romany blood doesn't run."

Then she looked directly at me, asked what I dreaded she would ask. She asked,

"Will you come with me?"

Ah, fuckit.

Less out of courage but more to not appear weak in her eyes, I said,

"I will."

She threw her arms round me and near shouted,

"Thank you, Jack, thank you so."

Everybody was hugging me these days, which made a change from them shooting at me though in some ways I was more comfortable with beatings.

Recently, I'd reread Donato Carrisi's *The Whisperer*.

Those lines hit me like truth,

"*You have to be careful with illusionists. Sometimes evil deceives us by assuming the simplest form of things.*" I thought of Sara and her Guatemalan blue light trick.

Sara posing as a child. What could be simpler?

Carrisi had added,

"*The details, the nuances, the shadow surrendering things, the dark halo in which evil hides*"

"The dark halo" described the aura of Sara to a chilling degree.

A Stained White Radiance.
James Lee Burke.

The above title suggested so many things, but mainly innocence corrupted and, for some oblique reason, it spelled out Malachy in all his misguided actions.

The very echo of those words reduced me to a state of lost despair.

Malachy's birthday was fast approaching, and I had to kill him?

Kill a priest, even if that's what he wanted?

I was forever *damned in troubled faith*, as the poet Ciannath De Brun had written. And damned in every spiritual fashion under a judgmental sky.

Why I drank.

Ceola had gone to chill in Oughterard, a tranquil place of cozy pubs and friendly locals. When she returned we'd head to Keefer's . . . and kill Sara?

A fierce amount of killing ahead and the weather was blistering hot—had been for three clammy weeks.

We Irish, we love sun, as we like anything scarce, like money, but with climate change Europe was baking, and London had Boris Johnson as new prime minister, who sacked all his opponents.

Calling him a buffoon, scandalizing about domestic battles, did not deter the fact that he was a *dangerous* buffoon.

I digress, as the lit gang says.

'Twas not the humanity but the freaking humidity that was busting our balls. We were beginning to buy fans and inquire about air-conditioning.

I met with Dysart, who also wanted to kill Sara.

Not a popular girl.

We were to meet in Naughton's, always called by the locals O'Neachtain's, the Irish lilt giving it a hint of Celtic smarm and, sure enough, you saw lots of ponytails, even on the women. I think I saw some tie-dyed clothing but I don't want to overwork the metaphor lest I lapse into bad poetry and qualify for an arts grant.

God forbid.

I was nursing a finely drawn pint when I saw Hayden, a crime writer of mid-list merit, meaning he sold fuckall. He had a clouded backstory of jail time in South America and carried an air of impending doom like a shadow of smoke.

We had met a few times, and got on well enough, neither of us borrowing money as is the mode in arty circles. He seemed to less like me than tolerate me.

He asked how I was.

I gave an Irish answer,

"Fair to middlin'."

He smiled, long familiar with Celtic evasiveness. I echoed,

"And your own self?"

He continued the Irish vibe with a question to a question.

"Do you speak Spanish?"

Like fuck, I mean,

"Seriously?"

I said with fierce conviction,

"Why?"

He was amused, not a neighborhood he much inhabited, said,

"I know you like quotations so I have a fine answer to your query."

He quoted,

"*Le gusta este jardin?*

Que es suyo

Evite que sus hijos lo destruyan!"

I saw Dysart approach. I asked Hayden,

"You want to have a drink with an ex-priest?"

He laughed and, as he moved away, said,

"Not even with a priest who isn't ex. See you again, Jack, and the quote is from Malcolm Lowry."

Dysart was dressed in black, like a mourning crow, the heat wave not on his radar. His face was drink-red and his eyes were slightly out of focus. Without preamble, he ordered,

"Double scotch."

He didn't offer me so I said,

"Bad hair day?"

He seemed to have made the mistake of cutting his own hair and had attempted the so-called buzz cut. It might have passed comment if he was an eighteen-year-old marine. He paid for the drink with a crumpled ten euro, ordered another. I said,

"Fuck sakes, easy."

He turned on me, snarled,

"Don't lecture me, Taylor."

I finished my drink, asked,

"You get my Seconal?"

He reached in his pocket, pulled out a tattered envelope, said,

"There's thirteen there. Should be unlucky for some poor bastard."

I took the envelope, put it away; to an onlooker it looked like a drug deal, which it was. He said,

"One hundred euros."

I asked,

"You take MasterCard?"

He looked like he might hit me, said,

"Do not fuck with me, mister."

I said,

"We're going to the country on Friday so pack your Glock."

Threw him. He mustered,

"Friday? I'm not ready. I need two days without booze."

I told him about Ceola, stressed the urgency of us going to the farm. I said,

"Here's the plan. Ceola, me, and, if you're sober, you go to the farm, take the girl without hurting anyone, bring her back here. I'll get in contact with Monsignor Rael. Let the Church deal with her."

He didn't like it, tried,

"Keefer won't let us."

I said,

"Ceola will persuade him. If not, we use the minimum of force, take her against his will."

He wasn't happy.

I said,

"Noon on Friday. Be ready."

I was leaving when a thought occurred. I asked,

"Why are you drinking like a lunatic?"

He said,

"To stop the nightmares of what I've seen of Sara's trail of terror."

I asked,

"Did it work?"

Sighed, as only the true, 100 percent blue alky can, said,

"Made it more vivid."

Thursday, the day before we went to the farm and, I hoped, as they say in the U.S., weren't about to *buy the farm*, I packed for the trip.

What do you need for a jaunt to the countryside to

Kidnap/kill a child?
Use force to restrain my best friend?
Rescue my falcon?

All you need is love?

Not really.
Just keep it simple.
A gun.
Your balls.
Lots of drugs.
Flask of Jameson.
Such was the plan.

I'd finally got time to meet with my wife—ex-wife—Kiki.

I hadn't seen her since our child was killed in my arms. At the funeral, she'd wailed,

"Why, why wasn't it you who died, you bastard? It's your fault my lovely girl is dead."

There was more but you get the drift.

She was now a member of AA so maybe forgiveness was part of her gig.

We met on neutral ground, the Meyrick, at the bottom of Eyre Square. It was fairly hopping as the Galway Races were to start on Monday. The heat wave was still in full merciless blast. I was early, nervous as a nun's cat.

I had dressed in order to not intimidate or provoke. She had always hated my lack of clothes finesse. I was wearing chinos, blue shirt, mocs. I looked like a geek's grandfather and felt it.

She arrived in heavy black, mourning for effect.

In deference to her AA status, I was drinking Galway sparkling water—even had a slice of lemon to whip up the bitter atmosphere hovering.

I stood to greet her, she snarled,

"Don't even think of hugging me."

Gotcha.

She told the waitress she would have chamomile tea.

'Course she would.

She sat, tentatively, cleaned the seat with medic wipes. I couldn't begin with

So how's the crack?

I tried,

"You wished to see me?"

She leveled her eyes at me; hatred burned her eyeballs, and didn't do mine a whole heap of good either. She said,

"I'm bringing Gretchen home to be buried. I want her gold miraculous medal back. You don't deserve it."

How could I say

"The devil child stole it?"

Like that would fly.

Thinking I hadn't quite heard her, she repeated the awful words.

"I'm taking Gretchen away."

Like fuck.

I said,

"You can't do that."

She laughed like a banshee, said,

"I've already had the paperwork done. She will be disinterred today and flown home tomorrow."

My turn to snarl. I went,

"No fucking way."

She pushed home.

"My lawyer already described you as a washed-up drunk and—guess what?—the judge knows you and despises you so you're screwed, mister."

Weak, like close to passing out, I pleaded,

"But she's all I have. What will I do?"

She stared at me for a long-tensioned minute, then,

"Drink. It's your life."

My heart was pounding. I implored,

"Oh, please, Kiki, please."

She stood up, victor triumphant, said,

"You never held her until the day you had her by the hand and let that man shoot her. It's your fault she's dead. *You, you* killed her."

I felt a tear roll down my face, *plink* in the sparkling water. I begged, truly begged, ended with

"That day, that awful day, we really bonded, we connected, I swear to God."

She was walking away, threw out,

"One day is not connected, it's bogus affection, meandering sentimental horseshite. She meant nothing to you and you mean even less to me. I ordered you a large whiskey to be served when I leave. Oh, don't worry, it's paid for, as is everything in your evil existence, paid for by others. Keep the miraculous medal. It's already tainted by your hands."

Then she was gone.

The drink appeared in jig time.

What did I do then?

I complained about the ice in it.

In Jameson? I mean, c'mon.

The next six days are lost to nigh total blur.

It was the Galway Races; you could do blitzkrieg drinking and still blend into the engulfing insanity of the week.

Many days later I came to in my own bed, had a tattoo on the inside of my left arm. It was a dove with *3.5* printed underneath.

I had what looked like a busted left cheekbone.

My face was covered in dried-out blood, bruises already fading, torn lips, upper teeth broken.

And lo, a miracle of Galway, maybe even a fucking epiphany: a duffel bag stuffed to the brim with fifty-euro notes, blood on the top layer, lots of blood.

I was wearing a newish T-shirt that featured the logo:

> Don't sweat the small stuff
> They too deserve to live.

Really?

It took two pints of water, two multicolor vomits, three aspirin, three fingers of Jay to be able to function, then a Xanax to measure me out, focus a little bit.

I did a scan of the room, no bodies immediately found.

My Garda jacket was hanging on the back of the door, the apartment wasn't trashed. It might even have looked tidy! Nobody likes a messy drunk.

"I'm not necessarily
Saying I go to a lot of funerals.
(I do.)
But
What does it say about
A man's life
That he has the undertaker
On speed dial?"

(Jack Taylor, the Galway Races, July 2019)

I checked the calendar. I'd been MIA for five days.

As I sipped the coffee, added a hint of Jay, I finally got the courage to check my phone.

Fifteen messages.

Took a deep breath.

Two from Ceola, the first berating me for not turning up to meet her, the second saying she and Dysart were heading for the farm and she hoped maybe I had already gone ahead.

A message from Malachy, saying,

"You were supposed to kill me two days ago and, what, you couldn't even rise to a birthday card? Would it have been so difficult to do that? Some friend you are."

Okay.

Then two from Dysart, calling me a cunt, demanding I show up. Another from Ceola. She sounded hysterical, scared, nigh screaming, like this,

"*God, oh God, Jack, this has gone very bad, oh no!*"

Then her phone went dead.

The rest were from Owen Daglish, urgently demanding I get in touch.

I rang him with a deeply ominous dread.

He opened by launching into a severe bollocking, then roared,

"Stay put, I'll be at your apartment in jig time."

He was.

He stormed in, asked for a large Jay, urged I have one too.

Looked at me, added,

"One more for you."

He lit a cigarette, blew out a cloud of tense smoke, said,

"There has been a massacre at the farm of your buddy, the Rolling Stone guy."

He let that hover, snarled,

"Where the fuck have you been?"

I didn't want to hear him say what my mind conjured up. He said it fast.

"Your friend is dead, a young lady who I believe lived with him, she's dead, and a man we have identified as an ex-priest and, weirdly, a falcon."

I asked,

"No teenage girl?"

He was furious, went

"Girl? Christ, aren't there enough dead for you?"

I said with an audible tremor in my voice,

"There was a girl of maybe fourteen staying there, the miracle girl, Sara?"

He said,

"Not the fucking miracle kids again. They have been a bloody curse."

How right he was.

Slowly, he described the scene.

Keefer with his face shot off. Ceola, her throat cut.

Dysart was burned alive when the farmhouse was set ablaze. The falcon was beheaded.

Forensics was treating it as some sort of bizarre murder(s)-suicide.

I put my head between my knees and vomited onto the carpet.

For a week I was put under the Garda hammer.

Questioned.

Quizzed.

Threatened.

Cajoled.

My answer to everything was constant:

"I don't remember."

And I didn't.

Melvin Minkler, now a senior officer, snarled,

"You're telling me you were in a blackout for *a week*?"

I looked at him. I was so shattered he could have beaten me to pulp (which he sure seemed inclined to wish for) and it wouldn't have touched the pain I was in. I said,

"No, no, I'm not telling you that. I'm telling you I don't remember. It could have been five days, six?"

He threw up his hands in exasperation, said to the young Guard taking my short statement,

"You fucking believe this cunt? He's admitting he's such a drunk he was out of it for days?"

The young Guard, named Sweeny, I think, said in total sincerity,

"I believe him. My dad was like that."

Melvin was enraged, went with

"Did I ask for your fucking family history? You think I give two shites about what your father does?"

Sweeny, undeterred, said,

"Does? No, did. He died screaming in the jigs."

When I was released, alibied by most of the barmen in the city, I leaned over O'Brien's Bridge, lit a cig, despair waltzing through every slow membrane of my beaten mind, and grief like a pounding blast of heavy metal hammering on every nerve.

A man approached, dressed in a fine white shirt, black pants with a crease (who irons anymore?). He was in his late fifties with short, neat brown hair, heavy black shoes. Despite the heat wave he had an aura of black anger. I know. I've been there often.

He near spat,

"You Taylor?"

I said,

"Unfortunately, I am."

He had spittle at the corners of his mouth, said,

"I'm Mister Haut."

Prick.

You call yourself *mister*, you obviously never had a real punch to the face, but it wasn't too late.

I said,

"And?"

He literally quivered, managed,

"The name means nothing to you?"

I lit another cig, tasting nothing, said,

"Nope."

His hand shot out, grabbed my shoulder. I said,

"Two seconds before I break your nose."

I didn't feel angry, not even remotely stirred up, but I would break his nose.

He pulled back his hand, said,

"My daughter, Greta, you threatened her, claimed she was a troll, the cause of a young woman's distress."

Took me a few seconds then,

"*Distress*? Fucking distress? Your bitch daughter hounded and terrorized a young girl named Meredith so much that she hanged herself with her dad's tie."

He backed away. I followed, consumed with rage, murder aflame in my heart, tears in my eyes, I shouted,

"*Distress, talk to me of that!*"

I looked at the bridge, warned,

"You say another fucking word to me, just one, and I'll throw you over that bridge and then I'll go to your fucking home and have another chat with your dote of a daughter."

He was moving away, said,

"You'll pay, Taylor. I'll see you will."

I got home, reasonably sober.

The young Guard Sweeny had followed me after I'd been released, asked,

"You okay?"

I asked,

"This good cop/bad cop?"

He sighed, said,

"I just wanted you to know that I was at the scene of the killings and I'll never forget the burnt horses."

Jesus H.

I said,

"What?"

What fresh horror now?

He said,

"The horses were doused in petrol then set on fire. People saw them in flames streaking through the fields, giving a sound that one man said was like the demons of hell had been released."

I had to lean against a wall, my eyes spinning in my head, images as if from William Blake careening round my mind, a nightmare that I'd never unsee nor unhear.

I thanked Sweeny for his concern, said,

"You're too decent to be a Guard."

He gave a sad smile, said,

"You'd know."

* * *

I rang Malachy, not knowing if he was dead, but he answered, snarled,

"You fuckhead!"

Hung up.

Went better than I'd hoped.

I met with Owen Daglish, tried to convince him that Sara was behind the massacre at Saoirse Farm. He was sipping from a pint of Guinness that had a creamy head it seemed a damn shame to disturb, but needs must.

He put the glass down slowly, didn't look at me, whispered,

"You need to see someone."

I was easing my sick soul into a Jameson, said,

"Right, right. I'm seeing you, telling you."

He gave me a long look, said,

"The week you were MIA, a drug dealer was robbed, someone gave him a beating and cleaned out his money."

I wondered,

Me? The bag of money?

He shook his head, as if the whole world was skew-ways. I asked again,

"Sara, the girl?"

He did something that underlined his despair of me. He pushed the pint away, said,

"You're sick in the head, Jack. You need professional help."

Walked away.

* * *

At a loss, I walked my own self, had finished my drink. I was fucked but not quite. I nearly drank Owen's remaining pint but I had some standards, ragged and blown, but still.

Went to St. Nicholas Collegiate Church. The Protestant one. I felt a niggling guilt at entering there, Catholic guilt never fully dispelled. It was silent, which I loved, and I felt an odd rare peace, sat down, remembered the last time I was here, during the maelstrom of *Galway Girl*.

Then mourning a dead child, I'd found an old poem on faded vellum by Gerard Manley Hopkins. It had been uncanny in its lines, echoing the sorrow of the time, my time, not GMH's.

No poem this round but, as I lowered my head in my hands, a memory of my days at the Bish in Galway, not a prayer away from where now I sobbed in hopelessness, our English teacher, a spoiled priest, beating me over the knuckles because I couldn't for the very life of me remember one line of a poem.

The poem was "An Irish Airman Foresees His Death."

By Yeats.

Out of sheer tenacity, many years later, as a Guard on border duty, I'd found a tattered copy of Yeats's *Selected Poetry* in a derelict house we were sheltering in from out of the rain.

I memorized that poem, remembered it there in the Protestant church.

I recited the lines under my breath.

They were scant comfort but the music of the structure was almost soothing.

* * *

I passed a guy who was wearing a T-shirt with a quote by the late Robin Williams:

> "If it's not one thing
> It's
> My mother"

Elicited a tiny smile from me. You take any trace of humor where you find it—even from a T-shirt.

The heat wave we'd been enduring rather than relishing was in its fifth week; the humidity was intolerable. Not that the vexed humanity was tolerable either.

I came out of the church to torrential rain, absolutely dashing, muttered the title of the very first Dennis Lehane book I'd read,

> *Prayers for Rain.*

Hard to blame Dennis, I guess.

I balanced all,
Brought all to mind,
The years to come
Seemed waste of breath,
A waste of breath
The years behind
In balance
With this life,
This death.

(W. B. Yeats, "An Irish Airman Foresees His Death")

I was at my apartment, trying not to think about

My deep friendship with Keefer.

The touching strength of Ceola.

The determination of Dysart.

The fierce beauty of the falcon.

The utter fear of the horses.

As distraction, I counted the money in the duffel bag, came to nearly 20,000 euros.

I sat back, went,

"A miracle?"

The doorbell shrilled.

More Guards, I figured.

Nope.

Monsignor Rael, the Vatican fixer.

He was dressed in a light black suit, immaculate white shirt that kind of glowed, his hair neatly cut, thin gold glasses, and his face like a shard of ice. He asked,

"Might I come in?"

Sure.

I waved my hand to signal *suit yourself.*

He came in, moved to the window as many did, and gazed at the expanse of Galway Bay. Then he said, without turning,

"We have us somewhat of a clusterfuck."

I lit a cig, said,

"You think?"

I asked,

"Drink?"

He turned, adjusted his glasses as if to scrutinize me more fully, said,

"Indeed, how hospitable of you. Black coffee, please."

I got that as he studied my bookshelf, said,

"Somewhat eclectic taste. Beckett next to Becky Masterman, Rilke next to a bio of Neil Young."

I said,

"What can I say, I'm nuts."

He smiled that thin smile that bespoke nastiness.

He said,

"Our chap Dysart, he was, I imagine, less than candid with you."

I had to be careful not to pick up the jagged tempo of his speech. It was contagious, like a disease, a faint mocking tone leaking over his words. I asked,

"Pray tell."

(See what I mean?)

He indicated the armchair, raised his eyebrows. I said,

"Sure, get comfortable."

He did, even if comfort was not really in his catalog. He began,

"The girl/woman, Sara, is not an orphan. She was born to the remnants of a cult who worshipped the cobra, on the run from authorities in the U.S. and U.K. They settled in the south of France briefly, where Sara was born, then some of them fled to Guatemala with the girl. Needless to say, they were not exactly model citizens and rumors about dark acts were numerous, but they had one vital ace, money, lots of it, and some government ministers were not disinclined to participate in their doings, especially child abuse and any sordid activity involving sex and drugs. But eventually they got bold, went too far, and a death squad wiped out most of them. Sara blended into the train of refugees fleeing the country. She had quite the reputation for tricks of light, languages, and a predator's skill of camouflage. But a bloodlust appetite would always surface and a number of bodies of young boys lined her passage."

He took a sip of the coffee, went on.

"Ouch, bitter."

Of course.

He said,

"She is incendiary. If she goes public, as well the crazy bitch might, the Church will be deeply compromised. I can see the headline: 'Miracle Girl Goes on Murder Spree.' We can't let that happen."

I said,

"I know where she's going."

He was astonished.

He lit up, asked,

"Good man. Get us something stronger to celebrate, you'll be full rewarded from the Church, my man, and you're gold."

As I poured two stiff Jays, he looked like he might hug me, God forbid. He stood, we clinked our glasses, and he said,

"To the inscrutable Mr. Jack Taylor."

I let him savor the moment, then I hit with the rider, said,

"Before I reveal her whereabouts, I need something from you, from the Church."

His smile lost some luster, but he gamed on, said,

"Name your figure."

I let the drama build, then,

"I need a week in one of your hideaways, the houses where you stash the wounded priests, the fallen, and, if you deny having such, all bets are off and you can, as they say in the best churches, go fuck yourself."

He sat back down, considered, then chuckled, said,

"Haven, you can stay in the Haven, and it's just down the road so to speak."

I was a little surprised he caved so easy, then pushed,

"I need to be left alone there, with a course of Valium for the duration."

He said,

"We can manage that. May I ask why? Not the Valium but the need to go there at all."

There were many bullshit reasons I could offer but I decided to go with the truth, see how that tasted, said,

"I am shattered." My mind a whirling cesspool of

Burning horses.

Murdered friends.

Mutilated falcons.

"And I am bone sick to the point of falling down. I need a week to be, if I don't sound too much like an asshole, *still*."

He mulled that over. I expected some sarcastic reply, got this:

"Burnout. I get it. I've been there. Few years back, when we first heard rumors of Sara, I followed a false trail that revealed horrors involving children and I lost it, my mind shut down, I was a walking basket case."

"Did you go to the Haven?"

He gave a bitter laugh, said,

"Yeah, right. The Church is not big on compassion for its, let's term them, *dark ops team*."

You might think we'd have bonded over our shared trauma but, no, there was something slithery about him. But I did concede,

"You're okay now, I guess?"

He gave me a calculating look, then,

"I read Deepak Chopra's *The Seven Spiritual Laws of Success*."

I could get a copy in Dubray's or Charlie Byrne's. I said,

"It helped a lot, then?"

Another chuckle with a definite overriding of nastiness. He said,

"To quote a Galway philosopher, *like fuck*."

I did warm somewhat to him. I showed him my arm, the tattoo of the dove, the figure *3.5*, asked him if he had any idea what it meant.

He took my arm, peered intently, asked,

"You got a tattoo and you don't know what it signifies. Jesus, you do need the Haven."

I lamely offered,

"I was drunk."

Now he gave a full deep amused laugh, said,

"If you get a tattoo every time you're drunk, you'll have more of them than David Beckham."

My bonding, albeit small, was gone already. I snarled,

"You know or not?"

He let my hand go, wiped his glasses like Richard Dreyfuss in *Jaws*, said,

"We're going to need a bigger boat."

Saw the anger in my face, apologized.

"Sorry, I just love that movie. The dove is, I think, to represent the Holy Spirit, the *3.5* is from Proverbs. *Trust in the Lord*."

Fuck.

I said,

"I can see why you love *Jaws*; you're the spit of the main character."

He was chuffed, beamed, asked,

"Really, Robert Shaw?"

I allowed him to savor, then answered,
"The great white."

So it was arranged. I'd be picked up in five days by Father Pat,
the former driver of Malachy when Malachy had been bishop-
in-waiting. When he was demoted, he lost not only his dignity
but Pat, who had turned out to be a smart little bollix despite
initially acting like a religious prick.

I'd given Pat a taste for Jameson and he was now a daily
devotee.

God knows, I've ruined many a priest, as indeed priests have
ruined many a man.

I needed five days to attend funerals: the deaths from Saoirse
Farm.

Ceola's father had turned up and taken her home to Scotland
to be buried under Ben Nevis. She'd like that. She might hear
the melody of violins along the wind from Edinburgh.

No one claimed Dysart. He was to be consigned to that in-
dignity I recalled from a bitter Irish past of

Magdalene laundries.

Tithes.

Rent men.

Evictions.

Pauper's graves.

Not if I could fuckin' help it.

And I didn't even like him but a poor man's burial, no.

Took some maneuvering but eventually I was able to get Joe Irwin—I can't say *my undertaker*, lest I draw witchy drama on my own self. Plus, I had twenty large to splurge so burying Dysart with class wasn't a stretch. I donated another wedge to the Simon Community.

I bought a new pair of 501s.

It is said
That an epiphany is most likely to occur
In a cemetery
Though
It helps
If you're
The mourner
Rather than the deceased.

(the journal of Father Malachy Brennan, 1952–2019)

Tuesday, another biblical rain lashed the hell out of us. In Rahoon Cemetery, I and Father Pat were the sole mourners, participants at Dysart's burial.

We were seriously drenched. This was ferocious rain like it had an attitude, a mission to drown us. Pat asked me if I'd like any special words.

I showed him my tattoo.

He was smart but not always, asked,

"You want me to say *dove*?"

I said with heavy patience,

"It's Proverbs, look it up."

He was still dithering, asked,

"Should I google it now?"

One of the gravediggers, drenched beyond ever dryness, chipped in,

"C'mon, fuck sakes, have the theological debate later. Can we just bury this poor bastard?"

We did.

The gravediggers shuffled off, muttering. Father Pat, rain dripping off every inch of him, asked,

"Were you very close to the deceased?"

I said,

"Actually, I disliked the fucker intensely."

By the gate, a man was standing forlornly, asked,

"Jacques Taylor, *n'est pas?*"

Though well covered in rainwear, he looked defeated. I said,

"*Oui.*" (No Irish person can answer in French without thinking *wee* and being faintly amused as well as feeling ridiculous.)

He said,

"*Je suis très désolée.*"

I had pretty much reached the end of my French fluency unless I tried, *Voulet vous coucher avec moi,* which would be insanely inappropriate.

The man said,

"*C'est mon frère.*"

Father Pat trailing behind me translated.

"That was his brother."

I wanted to say a myriad of things, all angry in nature, like,

You turn up the fuck now?

Where's your raincoat?

Speak fucking English.

Who cut your hair?

All reflecting the utter madness I was dancing along the rim of. He dispelled one of them.

By

Speaking English.

Said,

"Thank you for burying my brother."

After Irish funerals, we invite the assembled to partake of refreshments, meaning free booze, but as we were composed of three people now, or five if you included the drenched grave-diggers, I said,

"Come on. I'll buy you a Pernod or something."

Pat demurred, citing a Mass he had to say. I took it reasonably well, said,

"Don't be a prick."

I paid the gravediggers, added rain money, and the alpha of the two said,

"Gee, breaking the fucking bank here, are we?"

I added another fifty euros. He looked at it, said,

"Wow, now at last I can retire to the Bahamas."

We went to Kennedy's on the square. It's usually a hopping pub but the ferocious rain had kept even the hard-core patrons home.

We got a table. I asked our cortege what they wanted. I glared at Pat, cautioned,

"Don't even think of frigging mineral water or such shite."

He didn't, said,

"Hot Toddy."

I ordered three large of those and pints as outriders. The French guy was named Henri. I said,

"Henri is a name despised in Ireland."

He looked puzzled and not a little afraid. I explained,

"*Henry*, his handball kept us out of the World Cup."

He was baffled, tried,

"But I know, um, nothing about football."

I said,

"You're French. It's your fault."

He looked to Pat who was already deep in his hot whiskey and liking it a lot.

Pat protested.

"You cannot be serious. Blame every French person for Henry?"

I gave him the look, let harsh leak over my tone, said,

"We take our football very serious and don't even get me started on hurling."

I offered a toast, said,

"To Dysart, a holy terror."

Henri looked to Pat, who said,

"It's related to holy show."

As if this cleared anything up, Henri drank a hefty drop of the pint, smiled at the sheer quality of it. Kennedy's does one of the best.

Henri told us of the years of estrangement between him and his brother, and impressed me by quoting Philip Larkin, with a French take on Larkin's

Families, they fuck you up.

I considered that, said, as if I knew what I meant,

"The placement of the comma is vital to that sentence."

He smiled, said,

"Voilà, Lynne Truss is available in French."

Back in the days when I first met Father Pat, the days of *Galway Girl*, I had introduced/converted or maybe fucked the poor man's life by getting him to drink Jameson. Whatever, he took to it like a veteran and it made him bold. He now asked Henri,

"Why'd he get thrown out of the priesthood?"

Henri was taken aback by the bluntness of this but managed, "Drink."

Succinct.

Pat was not convinced, pushed,

"There's more than that to it. If they kicked out priests for drink, there'd be very few in the country."

Henri was not offended. Drank his pint, then said,

"My brother was obsessed with this girl/woman Sara, believed she was the reincarnation of the Sara from Camargue. It made him careless, stupid even. After he encountered her in Guatemala, he believed she was evil incarnate and demanded the Church warn people about her.

"The Church does not take kindly to threats and especially if they come from within the family, as it were. He was warned to stay away from her.

He didn't, confronted the girl, then, in a fit of rage . . ."

Pause.

"He threw a rosary at her and the cross scarred her just below her left jaw."

He looked at me, asked,

"Where do you place the comma in the life of my brother?"

Henri left us after that. Pat was all for me and him continuing a pub crawl but even I, who'd drink with most anybody, didn't have the stomach to listen to the drunk ramblings of a young priest.

I did ask him to check on Malachy and he stunned me by saying that Malachy was in hospital, gravely ill. Apparently he'd accidentally overdosed on medication.

I staggered away, tried very hard not to throw myself in the canal.

Before I got to my home I ran into Brigit Ni Iomaire, Ridge, same name as my dead Garda friend. That should have been warning enough not to stop.

But stop I did.

Brigit was supposed to have *the sight*, the ability to foretell the future. I'd known her a long time and had always given her a healthy sum of money. She seemed to like me okay.

Or

The cash.

Split the difference. I gave her a fistful of euros, she smiled sadly, said,

"Ta gra mor agam leat a mhic (I have great love for you, son). Ach to bronach agam (I am sad), mar tha do bhas ag teacht (your death is coming)."

I thought,

Fuck me.

She held out a thin bracelet of green Connemara marble, wrapped it quickly around my wrist. I said caustically,

"And this will save me, I suppose?"

She sighed deeply, stared into my face, whispered,

"No."

I took more of the found money, walked along Shop Street, and gave notes to anyone who asked me. Did this make me feel blessed?

No.

Next morning, I was woken early by the phone. My head hurt but then it nearly always did. I managed,

"Yeah?"

Heard a very cheerful voice go,

"Mr. Taylor, hope I didn't wake you?"

I snarled,

"You did."

A beat, then she continued, an American I guessed from not only the cheer but the accent.

"I'm Skylar Morgan of Morgan, Anderson and White and I have some rather good news for you."

I doubted it, said,

"Does it include dialing down the fucking fake delight?"

An intake of breath, but she recovered.

"May I call you Jack? I feel I know you."

I said,

"You don't know me."

Another beat then she forged ahead.

"You are the recipient of a large bequest."

I dropped the attitude, asked,

"How?"

She didn't feel comfortable discussing it on the phone so I got her address and said I'd be right over. The office, rather offices, were near the Skef on Eyre Square. Very impressive conjoined buildings, all large windows, modern facade, implying cash and lots of.

I was dressed like a bum, which is pretty much how I felt. Any thoughts of how I looked to people were over. I did wear the new 501s but they didn't appear to dazzle many. A secretary who could have moonlit as a model and probably did offered me coffee and a blow job.

Kidding.

A few minutes of the required waiting time to demonstrate your place in the pecking order, then I was ushered into a huge office, flowers, modern art covering the walls. Skylar was gorgeous but it seemed to be an office of gorgeousness in the middle of the city.

She made some polite small talk, then pulled out a file, put on a pair of thin gold glasses, made her even more lovely, said,

"So Jack, your late friend Keefer McDonald—and may I offer my condolences and that of my staff to you . . ."

Paused.

"Mr. McDonald has left you his farm and shares amounting to over one hundred thousand euros and his pickup truck."

Fuck me.

I nearly passed out.

Skylar fretted,

"Mr. Taylor, are you all right? You look . . . not too well."

I brushed that away, asked,

"Why?"

She sat back in her leather swivel chair, a fine smile creeping from her eyes, said,

"You saved his life, I believe."

Before I could even answer, she added,

"He had no relatives but he was a shrewd man, bought shares over the years. He told me he learned shrewd financial caution from Mick Jagger!"

She obviously didn't believe this, so I said,

"Jagger went to the London School of Economics."

I signed papers, gave my bank details, told her to put the ranch up for sale. Took the keys to the pickup. Thanked her profusely, headed out.

I stood on the pavement, trying to take this in. All the furious events, fierce changes that were hurling at me from every brand of karma. A guy stopped. I knew him from my days working security. If I was not fit to guard anything, he was worse and he got promoted.

He was one miserable fucker. He always, and I mean without fail, had bad news. He did not disappoint now, said,

"Your friend is dead."

More freaking karma but I asked, confused,

"You knew Keefer?"

He near spat.

"Who's he? I mean the dodgy priest you hung out with."

Malachy?

How did this asshole know? I asked him that. He sneered, said,

"It was on the news because he was in the running for bishop once."

I took a Vike, dry swallowed, stood at the top of the square, thought,

"Be powerful dope that could make me feel better."

Then along the very end of the square I saw the Madonna—the Virgin Mary—float before my eyes. I muttered,

"God almighty, how great is this Vicodin?"

Focused and saw it was a party of four men carrying a small statue of Our Lady. They were from an offshoot of the Marian Society.

I wasn't entirely sure if I was sorry or relieved that it wasn't real.

A family went on holiday to a remote part of the Malaysian rain forest for a holiday: three children, Irish mother, and French father. A girl, Nora, fourteen years old, with severe learning difficulties, shared a room with her siblings, aged twelve and nine. When the father went to check her room in the morning she was gone.

A massive search ensued with huge media coverage, wild speculation, and conspiracy theories. On the tenth day, Nora's body was found; she was naked, less than two kilometers from the hotel. A postmortem revealed, stated, she had died

From starvation and stress.

Photos of the little girl on the front pages of the papers, Nora looked so tiny, so vulnerable. You forced your mind away from the terror the poor mite must have endured.

I went to the Abbey church to light some candles for the child.

The doors were shut.

They were out of the church business.

I had no words for the impact of those locked doors. It was like a loud clanging shut of whole periods of my childhood.

An
Epiphany
Is
Frequently
Mistaken
for
a
Blessing

I was due to be picked up from Eyre Square to be driven to the
Haven.

I'd packed a pile of books.

Pairs of 501s.

T-shirts.

Two pairs of Doc Martens.

The OxyContin.

Underwear.

My hurley.

Two dozen old tennis balls.

My all-weather Garda coat.

And

Two bottles of Jameson.

Good to go.

I'm a child of generations of

Superstition.

Pishogs (unreliable sayings).

Belief in *seers, omens, signs, second sight, seven sons of seven sons.*

I know how pathetic this is but when you are hardwired to
this shite, it's difficult to shake. Now I saw a magpie, picking at
some shiny object under a tree, and I begged some deity.

"Let there be two, two for joy"

And phew-oh, a second arrived, thank God.

A car beeped me, my ride, as the Americans say, and we Irish think it is rude, to put it mildly, and just before I turned to get in the car a cat plunged from the branches, tore one of the magpies to shreds.

Monsignor Rael was at the wheel. I said,

"I'm surprised you're actually driving. Surely some lackey could have been used."

He gave a tight smile, said,

"We don't want the location to be known to mere mortals, and it's good for me to be out and about, among the plebes."

It was hard to tell how much of this he truly believed, but a hint of pisstake was in there.

He said,

"The Haven has currently five guests, all priests, and it's deemed diplomatic not to ask about the reasons for their, um, *stay*."

As we turned onto the Headford Road, he chanced a look at me, continued,

"The matron, Sister Martha, is a tough old bird, but she has agreed to your unusual requests, bizarre though they are. You'll be left to your own devices and how much you interact with the folk there is entirely up to you. She will deliver your daily dose of Valium every morning. She did stipulate that one week is as much as she can—how do I say this—*tolerate* your presence. It appears your rep is not unknown to her."

I weighed this, then asked,

"Bit of a cunt, is she?"

* * *

The Haven was situated near Lough Cong. Beautiful grounds, imposing front, like a grand hotel or holiday camp. We got out of the car. I said,

"Pretty big for only five clients."

Rael gave a sardonic laugh, said,

"We expect more, lots more, and more's the Irish pity."

We went inside and a tall nun in a severe black habit was waiting. She did a little curtsy before the monsignor, gave me a witchy look. Rael said,

"Martha, good to see you. This is Jack Taylor."

I was raised half right so I put out my hand. She looked at it like it was withered, kept her hands hidden in that cowl gig they use to intimidate. She said,

"Would the monsignor care for some refreshment?"

He wouldn't, said he had pressing business. I said,

"I could kill a gin and tonic."

Ice was her expression.

The monsignor turned to me, said,

"You'll be collected in a week and we expect an answer to our request."

He blessed us and fucked off.

Martha, without looking at me, said,

"Your quarters are ready: Follow me."

We went down a long corridor, passed two men playing chess. They didn't acknowledge us.

357

Just fucking fine with me, the rude bastards.

Martha opened the door to a bright large room, large bed, thick fluffy towels on the side, a scent of roses in the air. Martha said,

"This is en suite. There is a program on the table, times of meals, Mass . . ."

Pause.

"If desired."

Implying, the likes of me were far from Mass removed.

I decided to fuck with her a bit, said,

"Not exactly a Thomas Merton cell, is it?"

She turned her full razor vision on me, said,

"I don't like you, Taylor. I object vehemently to the *likes* of you being here, sullying our air. You keep out of my way, we'll get through this."

I asked,

"How will I know which of the men are the kiddie fiddlers?"

Being as crude as I could.

She took it like a lash. Her face steamed up and she moved forward as if to strike me. I warned,

"Touch me and the *likes of me* will knock you on your pious hypocritical arse."

She backed off.

I took out a bottle of Jay, muttered,

"The power of positive drinking."

* * *

The week went way too fast. I read, drank, chilled on Valium, and focused on Sara. Her preoccupation with the small village of Ballyfin. The plea from the parish priest there, for a *miracle*.

The village had tried to find an American politician to *discover* that his great-grandparents had once set foot in their village. *Any* politician; they weren't fussy.

Obama's visit to Moneygall made a fortune for that hitherto unknown place.

Trump's visit had revitalized Doonbeg.

Kennedy in his time had put the whole country on the map.

Reagan's visit had put another tiny village on the world stage.

Nixon, hmm, not so much.

Ballyfin would even have accepted Boris Johnson.

What they did get were refugees.

The government was facing strong opposition by proposing to plant refugees on unsuspecting towns and it had not gone well.

Ballyfin, so anxious for notice, had accepted a refugee camp on its doorstep without protest. The small village was suddenly packed.

A day of prayer to welcome them was proposed for September 1. The Church hoped to raise funds to restore the roof that was in grave danger of collapsing.

It sounded like a day to have a miracle.

It sounded like a day for a blue light trick from Guatemala.

It sounded like the perfect place for Sara to reinvent herself.

Ballyfin did have one rather odd claim to fame.

An ancient statue of Saint Patrick, not of great note itself, but his shepherd's crook they claimed was possibly the actual one he had used to drive the snakes out of Ireland. Fairly desperate, you'd think, but they did need that roof repaired.

I examined, recalled, every word Sara had said. She was a maestro at reinvention, and blending into a crowd was her modus operandi.

Refugees, a small village, a population desperate for a miracle. She would be in her element. But dangerous.

Always lethal.

At Haven I tried to take as much exercise as my body could endure. Long walks, sit-ups, push-ups, the plank exercise to stave off a beer belly.

I delayed drinking until the sun set, then eased into slow shots of Jay.

Control.

Control.

Control.

Read like a demented would-be writer.

Sister Martha left an envelope outside my room in the mornings with my daily dose of Valium, a pot of coffee. The meds kept the death of Malachy, Keefer, Ceola, my beautiful falcon at an artificial distance.

There was Mass each morning but I skipped that. I did eat in the dining room in the evenings. The other five "guests" kept their distance and I could hear their low conversation as if from a tunnel.

Like vague annoyance.

I caught one of the men sneaking furtive looks at me, curiosity without malice.

He was tall, with a lined face, as if he'd lived in the sun too long.

A missionary?

I was sitting outside, smoking.

My third day there, just counting the minutes until I went to my room, had the first of five Jamesons. He approached, asked,

"Mind if I borrow a cig?"

I looked at him, asked,

"When might you pay it back?"

He hesitated, considered, then,

"Tomorrow my stipend arrives."

I gave him a cigarette, fired him up, indicated it was okay for him to sit. He did so, carefully, as if all his joints hurt. I asked,

"They give you, like, an allowance?"

He nodded, shame hitting his body like a whip.

I said,

"Fuck that."

He gave me a long look, said,

"You're not one of us?"

I wanted to say,

You mean a pedo?

But he seemed in enough torment, and something about him was kind of okay in a very wounded, fucked-up fashion, as if he'd been decent once.

Was I judging?

You betcha.

I said,

"No, I'm not."

Meaning I'm not whatever "one of us" implied. He put out his hand, said,

"I'm Vincent."

I took it. Solid grip. I said,

"Jack."

He smoked awhile. I was not uncomfortable with that. I could do silence. He said,

"No offense but you have an aura of violence about you."

I laughed, not amused but in there, said,

"Unwise comment to make to a man you think is violent."

He mulled that for a time, then,

"I'm not a child molester."

Time to stop the polite shite. I snarled,

"Isn't that what they all plead?"

He literally sank within himself, let out a soft breath, said,

"Only two of the five here are that . . ."

Pause.

"That terrible term thing you're thinking."

I really could give a fuck. Few more days and I'd be on my merry way to kill a girl-child. He asked,

"Might I share some of that fine whiskey you have stashed?"

I thought about it, then stood up, went to my room, brought the bottle and a glass, one mug with Snoopy on it, sat, poured strong clerical measures, said,

"*Sláinte.*"

We drank. I asked,

"Won't Nurse Ratched be on your case for this?"

A thin smile, then,

"She's a nun. Nuns don't really chastise priests, least not openly."

I said,

"She's a nasty bit of work."

He laughed a little, said,

"Spite is her business."

I indicated the bottle and he nodded gratefully, said,

"I'm not sure I can recompense you."

Hah.

I said,

"When did priests ever recompense?"

Low blow.

Very.

He noticed my marble bracelet, asked,

"What's going on there?"

I told him about Brigit, her prophecy/foretelling of my impending doom. He was intrigued, asked,

"You seem an unlikely type to believe in pishogs."

I felt a flash of anger, a priest telling me not to believe in the very stuff his church relied on, even if they disguised it with Latin and pomp. I snapped,

"Did I say I believed it? Did I say that?"

He reeled back, the ferocity taking him from left field, tried,

"Whoa, *sorr-y*, obviously hit a nerve there."

The shithead.

"Sorry" was said in that passive aggressive tone that means sorry is the last thing they are. I was close to walloping him and he sensed that.

He was staring now at my recent tattoo, asked,

"Is that a dove?"

I dialed down the rage, said tightly,

"Yes, that's me, all about peace."

Sister Martha appeared like a banshee, like the worst of news. You didn't hear or see her coming. She glared at the Jameson bottle, ignored me, said to Vincent.

"Your meds and milk are waiting."

I held up the bottle, said,

"If you're expecting a shot of this, baby, you need to bring your own glass."

Fair dues, she didn't blink. Vincent stood, said,

"You shouldn't rile her."

I waved that nonsense away, asked,

"Your story, you owe me for the drinks, so spill."

He looked longingly back at the house, as if escape might still be open, but no, I'd stood up, so he sighed, asked,

"A last drink for the road, perhaps?"

I poured, was a wee bit shocked to see how the level of the Jameson had fallen, lit us the remaining cigs, waited.

He said,

"I listen to Joan Armatrading. Dates me, I guess, but her song 'Guilt' is the tune of my life. There was one of my parishioners . . ."

Paused.

"Maria Brady Nicoletta."

What a great name. Fuck, I'd date her my own self just for her name. I rolled it round my mouth. It fit, like fake joy. He gave a slight smile, knowing the power of the name, said,

"She deserved the name in that she was gorgeous, lovely in spirit, great heart, and . . ."

Longer pause.

"Married."

He looked at his empty glass then to me but we were all out of booze. He continued,

"I drank a fierce amount in those days. There was unease in my parish and, of course, with my *affaire*, lots of rumblings, but I was arrogant. I gave great sermons, not the usual dreary shite"—the Jameson kicking way into play here—"but real witty, uplifting material.

365

He stared at me, almost shouted,

"Get this. I wrote a weekly column for the local newsletter."

He blessed himself, shuddered at his recall, went on,

"God almighty, the shame. I titled it 'Clerical Errors' and used it to take shots at local businessmen. Then Valentine's Day, the fucking karma of it, I was driving Maria's Bentley, smashed it into a tree."

I guessed the rest, said,

"So Maria was in the passenger seat?"

He stopped, irritation in his eyes, said,

"No. No, she wasn't."

I could wait. He finally staggered out the ending, said,

"I never even noticed I'd hit a small boy *before* the tree. He died two days later."

Maybe in better stories, better people, I'd have given him a manly hug, muttered some inane bullshit, but I went with my gut, said,

"Your milk will be cold."

After he'd gone, I took the empty bottle, threw it in a wide arc, saw it disappear into the tree line. I shouted,

"Score one for Sister Martha."

In the morning Martha left me the paper, Valium, coffee. My hangover was about to kick in.

Hard.

But I stunned that sucker with the V, hint of Oxy, and the coffee. I wasn't kidding myself. These meds, hard-core as they were, would only postpone the inevitable crash. It would be a *muthafuckah*, as the brothers say.

I'd take enough of the Seconal I'd gotten for poor Malachy, sleep through the worst of it.

I hoped.

If I didn't wake,

Fuck it.

Mornings, I headed out to the large playing field with my hurley, the tennis balls. Whacked those fuckers out of the park. A scrappy terrier who belonged to the Haven watched me hit the first two. On the third I shouted,

"Go get it!"

He took off like the hound of heaven, a streak of utter speed and focus. Then he trotted back, delighted with his own little self, and dropped the ball at my feet. I had saved some strips of bacon from the kitchen, fed him one.

Then in perfect harmony I hit the balls and he hurled after them. A joy to watch a dog in full canine run. I didn't pet him, as I'd lost two dogs, and

Could not

Would not

Bond with another.

Midway, Vincent showed up, looking like a crushed nun, all wringing hands, guilt-pious expression. I said,

"Get yourself a hurley. We'll wallop that hangover to hell and back."

If you have depression, or just feel like shite, get yourself a hurley, stash of old tennis balls, a large field or, better yet, a spot above the bay, whack those babies out to America itself.

A dog is pure bonus.

Guaranteed to be the best vent you'll get without kicking the crap out of people.

I had to lend Vincent my hurley and what a joy to see him belt out years of rage into the blue beyond. He loved it.

Exhausted him and the dog. He exclaimed,

"That is awesome."

I asked him the name of the dog, he said,

"Novena."

He was drenched in sweat, rivers pouring down his body, and he was delighted. He said,

"'Tis a fine hurley."

I told him the truth. Sometimes it seems the thing to do. I said,

"My dad, the bed of heaven to him, went to an artisan in Bohermore, back in the days of the Magdalene laundries, and Rory Gallagher, the man took weeks to make individual hurleys from the ash. He'd put steel bands on the top if you were playing dirty bastards like Dublin. I've had it all these years and it's provided a measure of justice, if not the law."

I held it out, said,

"I leave tomorrow. I'd like you to have it."

Despite halfhearted protests, he took it.

That evening I stayed in my room, playing all the angles as to where Sara would be. Even tossed a coin. All spelled out Ballyfin.

In the morning, my rucksack at my feet, I said good-bye to Sister Martha. She said,

"Good riddance."

As the car approached, Vincent came hurrying out, handed me a well-read book. I said,

"Some spiritual horseshite, I suppose."

Looked at the title:

The War Against Evil (author unknown).

He said,

"In your case, it is indeed a spiritual battle."

The car pulled up, Rael driving. I got in, said to Vincent,

"Keep lashing those balls."

I did wonder after if it hadn't sounded just a tiny bit *gay*.

Rael drove fast, urgently, asked,

"Have you an answer for us?"

I lit up, blew smoke, said,

"Ballyfin. Next weekend she'll be there."

He nearly swerved off the road, gasped, asked,

"Isn't that the village with Saint Patrick's actual stick that he used to expel the serpents?"

I nodded. He mulled on that, that Sara would be there. Then asked,

"You sure?"

I was quiet for a moment, then said,

"I'd bet her dark life on it."

There's a moment in C. S. Lewis's *The Lion, the Witch and the Wardrobe* when the human children who have arrived in Narnia ask whether the White Witch, who rules the land, is a human woman or not.

The kindly Mr. Beaver tells them she isn't, and offers some advice.

"When you meet anything that's going to be human and isn't yet, or used to be human once and isn't now

Or

Ought to be human and isn't,

You keep your eyes on it

And feel

For your hatchet."

The Beast Slouches Toward Ballyfin

I had inherited Keefer's pickup truck as well as the farm.

The cynic in me echoed,

"I inherited the farm; he bought the farm."

Sunday morning.

Ballyfin.

There was a hatchet on the back panel, where in down-home Alabama there'd be a shotgun to *off any stray easy riders*. If I put on a Stetson, played Hank Williams, got me a hound dog, I'd be the redneck dream.

I drove to Ballyfin early. I heard on the radio that the celebration festival would be concluded with Mass outside the church whose roof they were raising funds to restore. People were advised to arrive early as the new influx of migrants would mean space might be limited.

Between the lines, you could almost hear a worry/caution from the Ballyfin residents that perhaps taking a hundred refugees was a stretch but for the day of fund-raising they'd suck it up.

I dressed in black for a black day: combat pants, sweatshirt, my Garda coat, and watch cap. I didn't have my hurley anymore but I did have the Glock.

Asked myself,

"Am I going to shoot Sara?"

On the pickup's sound system I played Dylan's "Sad Eyed Lady of the Lowlands."

Ballyfin was overshadowed by a large hill and the refugee camp was the other side of that, away from the village center. I got out of the truck, lit a cig, surveyed the camp. It seemed to teem with people—a hell of a lot more than a hundred.

I figured eco-warriors, do-gooders of all hue were among the throng.

A huge banner proclaimed,

SAVE THE AMAZON RAIN FOREST.

A smaller one behind near whispered,

LET'S SAVE THE CHURCH ROOF FIRST!

I asked myself,

How the fuck do I find Sara in there, if she's there?

Then I reassured myself.

She is drawn to crowds, needs a miracle, is fatally attracted to the glitz of a show, has the supreme arrogance of a predator who has never been stopped.

I went down to the church, managed to get past the crowds, saw the statue of Saint Patrick. The infamous *crook* was indeed ancient and the years had whittled away the tip so it resembled a spear more than anything else.

I thought I should maybe say a prayer but instead

I swore,

"Let's see about that bitch."

* * *

Most of the day I mingled among the ever increasing throngs of people.

Spotted two men.

I figured they were Monsignor Rael's goons/priests/hatchet guys. Near the fall of evening, as time for the Mass drew near, I saw Rael directing his team to spread out. He barked orders to the poor old parish priest, who seemed bewildered by so many people.

Then I saw a woman with a young boy in tow. I managed to get near her without her seeing me. She now had blonde hair, was dressed in some type of kaftan with dark jeans. She flicked her hair and I saw it.

The image of a cross burned into her neck below her left jaw and, shining in the late afternoon sun, a glint of gold—my daughter's miraculous medal.

The Mass was beginning and she hurried to the church, pulling the boy.

She entered the church. I was close behind. At the stairs, a sign warned:

DO NOT ATTEMPT TO MOUNT HERE. ROOF UNSAFE.

She flung the sign aside, hurried up, dragging the boy.

On the roof, she bent down, checked that the sky was dark, began to assemble her Guatemalan trick: blue light, cheap theatrics. She was intent on that, the boy near dozing at her side; doped, I figured.

I said,

"The show has been canceled."

She leaped back, stunned to be caught, drew in a breath, pulled out the serrated blade, spat,

"You."

I moved forward and she ran at me, spittle running from her mouth. The roof cracked, shuddered, and for a brief moment she was suspended in air where the portion of roof had been, then she fell, emitting a howl like all the anguished rage of hell.

I stood stock-still for a moment, then went to the boy, took his hand, gently, carefully took him down the stairs. He asked,

"Is she gone?"

I said,

"Yes."

His eyes sunk in his small head for a moment, then he said,

"Good."

The fall through the roof she might have perhaps survived but she'd landed on Saint Patrick, or rather his crook, been impaled. Her head was thrown back, her face almost gentle in death.

I handed the boy off to Rael's men, went back to Sara's body, Rael beside me. I reached over, snapped the gold medal from around her neck. Rael cautioned,

"That might be evidence."

I said,

"No, it's my daughter's."

He stared at the statue of Saint Patrick, then at Sara's left arm, which was thrown out from her. The cobra in that position seemed to have shriveled. Rael looked back at the saint, the saint who'd rid us of serpents, said,

"That's some irony."

I said,

"More like an epiphany."

I was drinking from my flask, watched as Rael summoned a car to take the boy away. He caught my look, said,

"Don't worry, he'll be fine."

Like a boy handed over to the clergy was in any way fine.

Rael saw my doubt, said,

"He'll be given a good home. I'll even send you the address when he's settled."

I accepted that bogus lie. Where could I take him?

Rael asked,

"You couldn't have taken her alive?"

I looked him straight in the eye, said,

"No."

As they were about to put the boy in the car I took off the green bracelet, handed it to him. He dropped it, spat on it, crushed it under his foot, said something I didn't understand. Rael looked to one of his men, who translated,

"He says magic is shit."

Back home, exhausted; if I'd been more sensitive I'd have *cried me a river*.

Instead I poured a large Jameson, downed a Valium, chased it with a Xanax (yeah, utter madness, but after the day of Sara what was sanity anymore?), then I lit a cig, read a poem by Kevin Higgins,

"The Reckoning."

Marked this:
My lungs are two talentless divas
Competing with each other for newspaper headlines
May everyone be arrested without warrant?
And made plead
Because my bill for life is on the mat
My lungs are rooms in which the yellow wallpaper is slowly falling
 down
My hates have come to get me

How apt would be "my hates have come to get me"?

The combination of speed, dope, booze didn't knock me out. Rather it took me out, out my front door and into town. I felt the desperate need of human contact.

What I got was Hayden.

The Hayden Epiphany

Hayden the crime writer.

"The mid-list guy."

As he so often said,

"Which means,

"I don't sell but do get some decent reviews and what they call *honorable mention*. If you see a collection of crime stories edited by a big name, they'll put the famous ones on the cover and add 'including others,' like the fluff tracks you find on an album with two big hits and eight duds."

He was, in most ways, an enigma. I'd said that to him and he near laughed, said,

"Right, I'm a half-arsed fact disguised as a dark rumor."

If I liked him, he tolerated me, like you would the last decade of a rosary you have to recite or get your knuckles walloped.

I met him outside Garavan's. He was dressed in his customary battered leather jacket, boot-cut jeans, trainers, and a T-shirt that was faded but still legible.

It read,

"Sorry

Me

Hole"

Have to be Irish to get the full lash/flavor of that.

Refers to a heroic man who confronted a fly tipper, videoed him dumping a rotten mattress, and the guy, realizing he was being filmed, said, *Sorry.*

Our hero answered with the above logo. It went on a T-shirt and went viral.

Hayden said,

"Lemme buy you that drink I keep promising."

We grabbed the snug in the pub, ordered boilermakers, and, as the young guns say,

"Chilled."

He began after we knocked the heads off perfect creamy pints.

"I've been reading like a reconnaissance fighter, reading

Joan Didion.

Marianne Moore.

Eudora Welty.

Charlie Byrne's is my vital support system.

Vinny, the star, gave me *The Enneagram*, a method of understanding your own self."

He paused, took a shot of the Jay, continued,

"Turns out I'm 'the Mediator.' The opening paragraph described how this type of child who, ignored by all, shuts down, *falls asleep*, knowing he matters little to others, especially in their family. They numb themselves."

He sat back. I said nothing.

Then, he went,

"That nailed me exactly and, in the modern usage of *woke*, prison woke me the fuck up."

Then he said,

"I need a smoke."

We went outside. He produced a pack of Lucky Strikes (where the hell he got them, fuck knows?), lit us with a battered Zippo, looked at the lighter, said,

"Craig McDonald gave me that, in Arizona, when we went to a reading by James Sallis."

He wasn't trying to impress me, just stating a fact.

I said what any lame bollix would say, I said,

"You were in Arizona?"

God almighty.

He laughed, said,

"I've always wanted once in my life to say the following, so here goes,

"*Well, duh.*"

I laughed. He had the keen Irish gift of undermining you with a simple jibe that sounded like warmth but was anything but.

He crushed the butt under his sneaker, said,

"Let's get another round."

We did, got on the bliss side of those, where the world seems cozy.

He said,

"Your turn, Hoss."

I feigned ignorance, asked,

"How d'ya mean?"

He grinned, said,

"Stories, we trade. You as the wankers say *share*."

Utter contempt spilled all over *share*.

Had to like the guy and I did, so I said,

"You're in the area of crime. How would you describe a teen-age girl/young woman/demon/psychopath?"

I laid out the whole saga of Sara, all of it.

He never interrupted, focused, took the odd sip of the Jay but otherwise was still. When I finished, he said,

"Pure evil, you'll find her in *People of the Lie* by Scott Peck, or Primo Levi, who in Auschwitz asked a Gestapo guard, 'Why are you doing this?' meaning the killing, torture, annihilation of a race."

He paused, as if he could see the very evil, and maybe he had, in South America. He continued,

"The guard gave the best answer to that I've ever heard and, believe me, I've searched for reasons my whole life. He said . . ."

Pause.

"There is no *why*."

With that showstopper, he stood, said,

"I've to bounce, as they say in *Breaking Bad*."

He looked at me, said,

"Bhi curamach mo cara (be careful my friend). I sense your narrative is ending and that would be truly an Irish pity."

He was gone and I was left like Padraig Pearse wrote in his poem
To ponder.

The Final Epiphany

I slept for two days solid. Did I dream?

Yes, of my father, who was walking away from me. No matter
how I tried, I could not catch up.

I finally got myself together, showered, shaved, clean clothes,
headed into town. I went to the best travel agency, with Annette
Hynes behind the counter.

She is one of those Galwegians who effortlessly make you feel
better than you are.

"Jack."

She smiled.

I told her I wanted to visit Camargue. Professional that she
is, she didn't ask,

"Why?"

She suggested I fly to Marseille, take a train to the seaside re-
sort Saintes-Maries-de-la-Mer. I said that sounded great, booked
it there and then.

Thanked Annette, headed for coffee, black, strong, and bitter,
I hoped. Got that in the GBC. Frank the chef waved to me. The
whole day was shaping up well.

After the horrors of the last months I was glad of any small
kindness.

Until.

Two young guys, dressed like *wiggers*—these are white guys acting like black men, the baseball caps worn backward, pants hanging round their arse, huge trainers, ultra-white, gold chains jangling.

I thought that annoying phase had died and been replaced by young guys adopting either

Peaky Blinders gig.

Or alas

The McGregor bad dude persona.

These assholes hadn't got either of the above memos.

Worse.

They were talking in what they thought to be the brothers' rap, like this,

"Shit just got real."

I figured I knew what it meant but it was so irritating to hear these fuckheads shoot it back and forth. What did I do?

Nothing.

Declan Coyle would be proud of me. His book *The Green Platform* proposed moving from "the red platform," rage, to a mellow state.

New to me. Very.

I was approaching the Wolfe Tone Bridge, stopped to stare at the horizon, heard,

"Hey, Taylor."

Turned to see Haut, father of the troll girl. He lunged at my neck. I felt a blade slice through the skin. I fell down and he continued to stab. I saw my hands awash in blood. I tried to count the stabs, managed,

"One,

Two?

No, there's more?

Is that

Four?"

Then I saw my father.

He was saying,

"*Shit just got real, Jack.*"

About the author

KEN BRUEN is one of the most prominent Irish crime writers of the last two decades. He received a doctorate in metaphysics, taught English in South Africa, and then became a crime novelist. He is the recipient of two Barry Awards, two Shamus Awards and has twice been a finalist for the Edgar Award. He lives in Galway, Ireland.